The Martian Job

NewCon Novellas

The Martian Job

Jaine Fenn

NEWCON PRESS

NewCon Press
England

First published in the UK by NewCon Press
41 Wheatsheaf Road, Alconbury Weston, Cambs, PE28 4LF
December 2017

NCP 137 (limited edition hardback)
NCP 138 (softback)

10 9 8 7 6 5 4 3 2 1

ISBN:

978-1-910935-61-3 (hardback)
978-1-910935-62-0 (softback)

Cover art by Jim Burns
Cover layout by Ian Whates

Minor Editorial meddling by Ian Whates
Book layout by Storm Constantine

One

'If you're listening to this, I'm dead.'

You have got to be kidding me.

That was what I thought, at that moment. Not: *Why is my brother getting in contact after all these years?* Not: *Oh no, Shiv's dead!* No: I was exasperated at the screaming cliché. Real people don't say melodramatic crap like that. But a cliché's just something that's been true too many times and one woman's melodrama is another's tragedy.

I paused the recording. My brother's smiling face froze.

I'd been given the chip less than an hour ago, when I dropped round to collect a box of clothes from the apartment. 'This arrived yesterday,' Ken had said in that neutral, careful tone he's taken to using with me. But we've been married long enough that I knew he was curious about the unexpected package, with its offworld customs sticker. I made like it was something I'd been expecting, but he saw through that, though he pretended not to. And I pretended I didn't notice him pretending not to.

Shiv's image stared up at me from my phone; I'd had to hire a chip-reader from the local cornershop-cum-pornbroker and it wouldn't talk to the screen in my hotel-room-cum-cupboard. The last time I'd seen my half-brother was on the vidlink from Ma's trial, when he'd looked stricken, silent and serious. On this recording he had more lines on his face but looked fit and well, with the same indefatigable smile, restless hands, breathless speech.

As I went to restart the recording I had an incoming call. Mr Lau. I took it, of course. He was most apologetic about disturbing my evening, but he'd just been notified of a delegation arriving from Beijing in two days, and they needed confirmation of the travel arrangements by lunchtime, their time. No need to go into the office, should only take up an hour of my time.

The chip had to be Shiv's idea of a joke, and it wasn't one I expected to find funny. Like a good little wageslave I put my life on hold and danced to my boss' tune.

It took an hour and a half to make the initial reservations. By then it was after midnight and I couldn't face dealing with Shiv's message. Tomorrow was threatening to be another long day. I should get some sleep.

But first, I went out to the loud and badly lit bar down the street, found a drunk young man with good abs and minimal conversational skills, brought him back to this pokey excuse for a room, and had a decent, if cramped, bout of meaningless sex.

My name is Lizzie Choi, and this is the story of how I became the most wanted person in the Solar System.

This was the second time in a month we'd had sudden notification of a visitation from Head Office: the massive gamble that was Project Rainfall was sending ripples through every part of Everlight.

In addition to the flights and hotels I'd booked overnight, the next morning I added chauffeur-driven vehicles, a private dinner at the Savoy, plus a selection of diversions for the three spouses and pair of teenaged children accompanying the half-dozen strong delegation. And far be it from me to imply this was any sort of jolly for said spouses and kids. Still, the Chinese do love London; the bits of it they don't already own, anyway.

By lunchtime, our time, everything was in place for the visit and I was ready to start my ten-hour work day. I asked Mr Lau if he was free to speak with me before he headed out for his lunchtime meeting. He invited me into his office, and greeted me with his usual avuncular smile.

'Another path smoothed. Thank you, Ms Choi.'

I smiled back. From where I stood, between his two plush visitor chairs, I noticed that the orchid stem in the lacquered vase on the southwest corner of his desk had a small brown blemish on the underside of the main blossom, only visible from this angle; I made a mental note to get it replaced before he returned from lunch. 'My pleasure as ever, Mr Lau. However, whilst your gratitude is my most treasured reward, current circumstances force me to mention the possibility I raised some weeks back, that of a remuneration review.' Or, to put it another way *You're not a bad boss but I need more money.*

His eyes went to the orchid. Perhaps the blemish was visible from his side. 'Your circumstances. Ah, yes.' Not a bad boss, but with an old-fashioned view on infidelity and divorce. 'I will see what can be done, given the current corporate climate, Ms Choi.' Or, to put it another way, *Fat chance.*

While Mr Lau was out at lunch an automated system called my personal phone asking if I'd accept a reverse-charge offworld call. I assumed it must be some mistake, then wondered if this was Shiv following up on his odd little joke. But it wasn't from Mars, it was from Luna.

If it was who I suspected it might be then this wasn't a call I could take at work, even alone in the office. I refused it. As I did so I realised there was only one reason my mother would be allowed to call me in the first place.

After years spent disentangling myself from the disaster that was my family, they were back in my life.

If Mr Lau noticed I wasn't at my best that afternoon he didn't say anything.

I got away from the office as early as I could. I needed to listen to Shiv's message all the way through. But my phone chirped again as soon as I was outside. I queried the call source. It came from Luna Authority Correctional Facility Six. She wasn't going to give up. I waited until I was back in my tiny room before bowing to the inevitable.

She didn't look that much older; a bit thinner in the face, but healthy and with her hair-colour back to glossy chestnut. Behind her the blank wall was painted a soft and non-institutional blue. 'Hello, Mother,' I said before she could open her mouth.

The Earth-Luna delay was only a couple of seconds, but it was enough for me to see her expression fall into the familiar combination of concern and disapproval. 'Beth! Been trying to get hold of you all day.' She sounded more American than I remembered; her only link to the old US was a single grandparent she'd never met, but everyone indulged the remaining Americans, so she'd probably been cultivating the accent in prison.

'I've been working. I can't take personal calls on work time.'

'Working?' The idea still appalled her, it seemed.

I resisted the urge to sigh. 'At Everlight, yes.'

'You're still with the opposition?' My father had called them that, jokingly; given how little time she spent with him, and how that time ended, it hardly made sense to refer to one of the world's biggest companies as 'the opposition'. But that was my mother.

'Yep. Still at Everlight.'

'Well fuck me.' Another thing about my mother: she loves to swear. She blames it on having had, as she puts it, 'a shit childhood' but I think it's more about image, the street-smart American shtick. And because she swears, I don't. 'And're you still doing,' she waved a hand dismissively, 'office work?'

'Operational administration.' After years of silence, and with a noticeable delay on the line, she could still propel me from mildly peeved to wound-up-fit-to-scream in a matter of seconds.

'And how's...' another hand-wave, 'whatsisname?'

'Fine.' I bit down on the word, but her eyes are narrowing.

She squinted past me. 'Thought you two had one of those neat corporate apartments.'

'You're calling because of Shiv, aren't you?' She would only have been allowed to contact me because I was now her registered next-of-kin. Because Shiv really was dead.

Her expression fell, and she looked old for the first time. The pain I glimpsed wasn't entirely faked. 'Yes. He... he was everything I could've wished for in a child.'

I let my subconscious chime in with *unlike you,* because I had no desire to be everything my mother could have wished for. 'When did he... When did it happen?' *My brother's dead. My brother's really dead.*

'Shit. You don't know?'

'No. How would I?' I didn't even know how he'd got hold of my contact details. 'I only know at all because of this call.' Not technically true, but I wasn't giving her any ammunition. 'So, how long...?' I let the question trail off into the signal-lag.

'Three weeks.'

In order to reach me when it did, Shiv's chip must have left Mars three or four days after it happened. Whatever *it* had been. 'And how did he...' I had to say it some time, '... die?'

'A flyer crash, according to some shyster Martian lawyers. He left details of his final wishes with them.'

The same lawyers who'd presumably found out where I was, and dispatched the chip. 'A flyer? He was a good pilot.'

'According to these lawyers it was a solo flight, and he didn't file a flight-plan with Olympus Central.' *You don't say.* 'They claim he ran into technical difficulties but that the glider's transponder had been tampered with. A rover-train spotted the wreckage two days later.'

In other words, anything could have happened. 'These lawyers, who are they?'

'Shah... something. No, Shah, Shah and something. What the fuck does it matter?'

'Probably doesn't.' Not a Chinese firm, then; no surprise there, either. Should I tell her about the chip Shah, Shah and something had sent me?

'But it ain't all shit, Beth. There's one piece of good news. His legacy, perhaps.'

Mum's so calm. But she'll have known about Shiv for a while. 'What do you mean?'

'It's coming up for ten years. Since I first came to this shithole, I mean.' Spoken as though she could leave. Which, I realised with a jolt, she could, potentially.

'You mean, the buy-out clause?' So that was why she was calling me. Not to commiserate on our shared loss, mend fences or volunteer useful information. No, as usual, she wanted something. Whatever was on Shiv's chip, I wouldn't be sharing it with her.

She nodded. 'I've had a decade to, as the shrink here says, reflect on the human aspect of the incident. Now I've done my time and had my therapy the slate's clean, of the whole culpable homicide thing anyway.'

The remaining ten years of Mum's sentence were a material loss penalty, which could be reduced by paying certain fines. 'The court set a ridiculous price, if you remember.' The vagaries of Lunan law: damaging a hab was as dire an act as taking a life, but if you could pay for a new hab to be built your crime need never be spoken of again.

'Yeah, they sure did. But you've done well, you said so yourself.'

I did? When, exactly? She was looking at me like she expected me to conjure the necessary funds out of the air. 'Not that well, Mum. Sorry.'

'Ah. So it's like that.' She sighed, and got that disappointed look in her eyes. I was still working out the best way to field this latest ploy when she continued. 'If you could, you'd free me though, wouldn't you? We could start again.'

'Of course I would.' What else could I say?

She nodded. 'Thank fuck for that at least. Sometimes, Beth. Sometimes I wonder about you, how you turned out. But you're a good girl really.'

'I have to go now.'

'Sure, I guess.'

'Bye Mum.' I cut the call.

I pulled the package containing Shiv's chip out of the cubbyhole where I'd stashed it. The chip was in a holder, the holder was in standard packaging along with a hardcopy slip of paper with the cryptic phrase 'Remember the world's dodgiest airlock?' printed on it; the package was labelled with my name and last registered address and a customs mark which indicated it came from Mars. And that was it. The piece of paper would have foxed anyone else; but as soon as I'd opened the package I knew what it meant, and who this package came from.

I should go out and hire the chip-reader again. Instead I decided to go out and get laid. Sex was, truth be told, the solution to a lot of my problems these days, even if it was also the cause of one of them. Which made Ken's call, as I was putting my lipstick on, perfectly timed. Behind my soon-to-be-ex-husband the apartment looked spacious, comfortable and airy. Still no signs of change, specifically the kinds of change made by another woman.

'I expected to hear from your lawyer today, Lizzie,' he said, doing that looking-up-from-under-his-brows thing I used to love but which I'd come to think of as passive-aggressive neediness.

He did have a point, though. I'd forgotten to call the divorce lawyer. I never forget things like that. 'I... had a difficult day.'

'You can tell me about it if it helps.'

I wish he wouldn't make civilised, genuine-sounding offers like that. Just like I wish there was another woman, or man, or something else; some other reason. He's trying to make this as easy as he can, and that just makes it harder. 'I'm fine. I'll get on it first thing tomorrow.'

The lawyer in question wasn't available first thing, so I had to queue the call for lunchtime. If I'd had the money I'd have hired a lawyer who'd return my calls, but the storage charge on those possessions I no longer had room for in my nasty little cubbyhole – which was most of them – had just gone out, and I barely had the money to pay rent on said cubbyhole. My original thought, that I'd get a studio flat in a nice, non-corporate suburb once the divorce went through, was about as likely as me taking Mr Lau's place as Everlight Europe's Junior VP for Finance.

I stayed for the meet-and-greet for the visitors from Beijing, hovering in the background trying not to look too tall and Western, on hand in case anything went wrong. Which it didn't, because I'm good at my job.

As soon as I got home I rented the chip-reader.

When my phone screen asked for a password, I keyed in DAE-BUM, the designation on the LunaFree Community's main cargo airlock. It used to make me laugh, especially the way Shiv said it, 'That's DAE as in Dodgiest Airlock Ever and BUM as in *bottom!*' What can I say, I was only eight.

The initial screen showed Shiv in freeze-frame, and a date. I hadn't really registered the date before but I now knew he'd recorded this three days before he died. I swallowed and hit play.

'If you're listening to this, I'm dead.'

Yes, you are. You really are.

'Just kidding! Got your attention though, didn't I?' He didn't look dead. He looked great. I blinked and his image went blurry for a moment. 'By the time you get this everything will be sorted. I'm stashing the chip just in case, well, in case two things, but mainly in case you don't work out it was me! Because it was!' He grinned wider, like he expected me to get the joke. 'Mum's probably free by now – that's one of Mr Shah's conditions for sending you this, me having bought her out. Which I will be able to afford because I've just pulled off...' his voice rose in that mock-gameshow-host way he had, '...the greatest heist humankind has ever seen!'

Except he hadn't; or if he had, it'd gone wrong and been hushed up. Plus: great idea this, Shiv – you're about to commit a fantastic bit of thievery which no one can pin on you, so you record a confession. Okay, it was on an encoded chip which – presumably – no one else had access to, but even so, that kind of arrogance could get you in trouble. Killed, even.

His expression fell, the smile fading a little. The back of my neck prickled. 'There's also a real small chance' – one of Mum's favourite phrases that – 'a real *real* small chance that things might not work out. That's why I've given you the details. Because if something unexpected happens and I can't do the job for some reason, then you could take it on. I know, I know, you don't touch this kind of business any more, you're on the straight and narrow working for the big bad corp, but you can't miss this one! And if I can't see it through then you've got to be the one who gets Mum out of that place.'

Oh, have I?

His moment of sombre reflection was gone as fast as it arrived, and the winning smile was back. 'I'm just being pessimistic. Everything'll go fine. And maybe, when the dust has settled, we can meet up? I know you still feel bad about how Mum got shafted in New Bombay and the Four Flowers business on Luna, but we're older now, older and wiser. And you're still my little sister.' He mimed blowing me a kiss, then blew a raspberry. His traditional farewell, back from when we were kids. 'Bye now!'

I threw my phone across the tiny room. It bounced off the wall. I retrieved it, and, because I had to pick the scab, checked the data-file. Sometime during Shiv's speech I'd got it into my head that his 'greatest heist humankind has ever seen' would be about Project Rainfall. That he was going to try and steal the water-rich proto-comet Everlight were currently braking into a stable orbit around Mars. I wouldn't have put it past him to try, given he'd trained as an engineer, back before he'd taken up the family trade. But I was wrong.

He wasn't planning to steal a comet.

He was planning to steal the most valuable gem in the universe.

I returned the chip-reader on my way out. Time to get laid again.

Two

Mr Lau spent most of the next day closeted with his visitors. It gave me far too much time to think.

Shiv had ended up on Mars eight years ago after a dodgy mining operation that went south when he tried to play the Russians off against the Australians whilst simultaneously screwing the Chinese – over-reaching himself, again – leaving him broke and under threat of multiple lawsuits if he ever came back to Earth. I could imagine him kicking around, moving from scheme to scheme in the Martian underworld (such as it was) waiting for the big break that was always just around the corner. When he'd been offered a chance to steal an object so legendary that Mum used to joke about it when we were growing up, something that in the shady world I knew too well was a byword for the ultimate score, of course he'd taken it, no matter what the risk.

I knew my brother. All that bravado was a front: Shiv had been scared when he made the recording. And his fear had been justified. I should just burn the chip.

When Mr Lau re-surfaced that evening, he looked harassed. I asked whether I could be of any assistance. He managed a smile for me and, in an uncharacteristic lapse in his façade, said, 'This project will make or break us all, Ms Choi.' I didn't have to ask which one. Since they wound up the last of their operations in

North America, Europe was Everlight's least prestigious division, run more for politics than profit. With so many eggs in one – off-world – basket, Mr Lau was fighting hard to keep hold of his small part of the corporate empire here on Earth.

I wondered if the universe was messing with me: I'd ignored Mars for most of my life, and now two things in one week made me think about the place. I dismissed the thought as unhelpful going on self-obsessed.

Even so, that night I did some research. Just background, I told myself.

The next morning saw more meetings, after which the delegation got to have a few hours fun before going home. Mr Lau's part in the visit was over and I was careful to give him space. He appeared, if anything, more uneasy than he had the day before; knowing him as I did I put this down to embarrassment at showing his concerns before an underling.

When he called me into his office 'for a private chat' I was more relieved than concerned. He was doing me the favour of telling me to my face that my pay-rise was off the cards.

He invited me to sit before he spoke. Not a good sign. This was serious. 'I am afraid, Ms Choi, that the situation is not favourable to you.'

'Ah.' I wasn't sure what else I could, or should, say.

'Certain factions within the company feel I should let you go.'

What? 'Really? I'm a great administrator and you know it!'

He raised an eyebrow at my immodesty, but said, 'You are exceptionally good at your job. Your attention to detail is remarkable, your foresight faultless. In operational office matters, I would not want anyone else to, as they say, *have my back.*' That last phrase was in English, which I knew from previous experience meant he was trying to put me at my ease.

'So what is the issue here?' I had an idea. I'd just been too busy worrying about everything else to join the dots.

He cocked his head a fraction. 'Some of my more traditional colleagues in Head Office put a high value on heritage. Specifically, on one's family.'

'Family?' I said, as though I didn't know. This wasn't just about me and Ken.

'Yes. You have criminal connections, Ms Choi.' His tone didn't accuse so much as observe, pointing out something socially awkward, like having spinach in one's teeth.

'Criminal connections.' I kept my voice flat. My original application to join Everlight nine years ago had included the usual box for listing any convictions; thanks to a mixture of luck and care, I had none. 'You're saying my family contains criminals.' There hadn't been a box for that.

'Yes. Your mother...'

'My mother?' Today's orchid was, I noted, perfect.

'You have recently become the registered next-of-kin of a certain Maria Kowalski.'

Of course Everlight kept tabs on their employees, and something like that would get flagged up. 'Yes. Yes I have. For my sins.' Lunan law allows you to divorce parents as well as partners, so if I'd had the money, I could've made the distance between me and my mother formal, rather than relying on our default state of estrangement. But I hadn't. 'I hope and believe, Mr Lau, that you can see beyond a person's initial circumstances to what they may achieve for themselves.' *Creep*, said a small, rebellious part of me I thought I'd excised.

'It would be easier to overlook these circumstances had you declared them when you first joined us.'

There *had* been a box on the application form to add Any Other Pertinent Information and I had agonised about using it to declare my 'criminal connections' at the time. 'My apologies, Mr Lau. I should have done so.' But then I probably wouldn't have got the job. Plus, it was just an office admin post and if they really cared they'd do a background check. I assumed they had, before I reached my current, somewhat more important, position. Apparently not. Or they had, but when Mum had no legal hold on me, they'd been willing to ignore her. My face felt hot.

'Suspension pending an investigation is the minimum you can expect, I fear. However, I will fight to the best of my ability to retain you as an employee of Everlight.'

I believed he would. He got good work out of me. And, for a half-gwailo, I made the effort to fit in. Which just made me more angry with the company, and with myself, and with Mum. And anger makes you do, and say, stupid things. 'Thank you.' *Don't thank him, creep.* 'Given the situation, I would like to request a formal sabbatical from Everlight.' Even as I said it, I was stunned at myself.

His eyebrows went up. 'That is an interesting proposition.' Then lowered, as his initial surprise settled. 'Possibly a sensible move though. How long would you wish to take?'

My subconscious had already done the maths. 'Three months.'

I like space travel. Granted it's potentially dangerous and often uncomfortable, and the cramped conditions on the cut-price flight I ended up on were grim, but I travelled enough when I was younger that I don't puke when gravity goes away, and I love the sense of going somewhere, towards something better, a place where things would go right. Mind you, when I was younger we were more likely to be running away from something that'd gone wrong.

Even taking the budget option, I had to sell most of my remaining possessions to buy passage to Mars. A return, because when I'd worked through this upwelling of the past I'd be back, returning to what was left of the life I'd built on Earth; by then Mr Lau would have smoothed things over, and be really missing his star admin, and I'd be able to go back to my old job. That's what I told myself, as I boarded the flight.

I should have spent the journey working out my options but

my thoughts just went round and round, tumbling in the near freefall, and coming back to two facts: nine years ago I'd decided to miss out a detail, a simple declaration on a form, and now it was coming back to haunt me; then a few days ago I'd acted on a crazy impulse, and in doing so risked undoing the chance at a normal life that form had bought me.

Stepping off the shuttle into Martian gravity, seeing people as tall as I was, gave a brief, comforting illusion of coming home. But this wasn't Luna. The sky beyond the dome was red, not black, and the air smelt of dust, ozone and something sweet – orange peel, perhaps?

By the time I'd queued for, and been crushed into, the lift down from the crater rim and queued for, and been glared at by, customs and joined the even longer queue for immigration, the scale of my potential mistake was sinking in. I was on an alien planet, with little money and no plan.

The walls in Arrivals were covered in the usual combination of adverts, infomercials and warnings about contraband and contagions. One image showed the Eye of Heaven floating, like some round shining god, over a hyper-real and lightly animated – or possibly real-time – depiction of the Olympus region, with the caption, *Peace and Prosperity For All*; the Everlight logo at the bottom left was subtle enough to miss if you weren't looking for it. On Earth, Everlight were a major player; on Mars, they were top dog. The last two decades had seen a meteoric rise in their fortunes on the red planet as every major decision turned out to be right, every gamble justified.

The Arrivals hall also contained discreet niches with actual gods in; the nearest contained a happy jade Buddha. The orange peel smell was stronger here: dry incense, for when you wanted to appease the ancestors without clogging the air scrubbers.

One wall had a flatscreen newsfeed – very retro, or possibly normal, for Mars – and I distracted myself by watching it while I queued. On screen, a thin-faced young man was complaining about Project Rainfall, saying Everlight had no right to hold people to ransom with the promise of rain. The comet's water belonged to all Martians, he insisted. Something about that phrase, 'all Martians', lifted my spirits. No one ever says 'All Earthers'. Okay, so Mars is just a bunch of semi-independent enclaves and habitats, as is Luna, but hearing someone speak like that made me feel warm and fuzzy inside. I just couldn't escape that early communal upbringing. As a caption appeared at the bottom of the flatscreen, I realised I wasn't so far from the truth: this was a spokesperson for the Deimos Collective. Somewhat ironic, talking about 'all Martians' when he didn't even live on the surface of Mars. Still, the Deimons did claim to speak for the ordinary folk of the planet below them and they had the height and weight – physically, morally, financially – to make statements like that. And the Chinese had the temporal power and self-assurance to ignore them. The queue moved, and I looked away.

Once through the formalities I used the public comm service to book into the cheapest accommodation I could find; it called itself a hotel but was more like a person storage facility, and made my accommodation back on Earth look downright spacious. Then I paid a visit to Shah, Shah & Needlam. I didn't call ahead in case the lawyers refused me an appointment, and I had to sweet-talk their receptionist and wait for an hour before I got to speak to Mr Shah, junior. He was predictably surprised to see me. When I made my request, his face fell further.

'Your brother's remains? I am sorry Ms Choi, but he had no stated religious beliefs or relatives in a position to collect said, ah, remains. Therefore he was, well…'

I knew the drill. 'He was resyked.'

'The phrase we use is "physically reintegrated".'

'I understand.' On Luna the official term was 'returned to the system'. I'd half expected this, and I wasn't sure what I would have done with Shiv's body or ashes anyway. But I had to ask. It was an attempt at what the Americans used to call closure. His final mark on the world.

It didn't have to be, of course.

Three

'Tea, Ms Choi? I have jasmine, green, chai or English.'

The available selection implied considerable resources, which was no doubt the point. But I hadn't had a decent cup of tea since I left Earth. 'English, please. White no sugar.' Though I preferred Western tea I usually drank Eastern teas in social situations, but I didn't have to worry about fitting in here. Besides, I was curious to see whether the perfectly turned out young woman sitting opposite me had access to cows as well as decent hydroponics.

She waved a hand at the boy who'd shown me into her office-cum-parlour. He drew back from the threshold, pulling the painted screen-door closed behind him. A subliminal hum started in the roots of my teeth.

'So,' she drew the word out with care, 'you are Shiv Neru's sister.'

'I am. And your own sister runs the Moonlit Joy Escort Agency?' I kept my tone lightly quizzical without being critical. Who was I to judge anyone by their family?

'She does. Using a back room in her premises provides additional discretion for my own business.'

'Which is what, exactly?' Shiv's recording had provided me with a name – Ika – a contact number – which I had done a directory search on, along with as much other research as I could without spending serious cash – and his assurance that 'Ika' was 'doing a great job of bringing everything together'. And that was all I knew.

'I am a facilitator.'

As I thought: a fixer with pretentions. 'Excellent. And what, exactly, were you facilitating for my brother?' I suspected she'd done more than facilitate him; she was in her twenties, mixed heritage (I'd guessed some Japanese from the name, but looking at her now I'd say mainly Indonesian), petite, stylish and possessed of a weaponised smile. Exactly his type.

'A unique endeavour which, I believe, you know something of?'

Did she know about Shiv's recording? 'Something, yes.' With a job like this you had to strike the balance between compartmentalisation and coordination. Tell your people everything they might need to know – but no more. When I say 'you', I mean the money. But Shiv wasn't the money. His recording had implied he was the brains behind the job, but a lot of the mental lifting, could be – probably should be – done by an individual like Ika. 'Before I go any further, I'm afraid I'm going to have to ask some direct and searching questions.'

Ika's expression tightened, but she simply said, 'I would expect nothing less.'

First things first. 'Did you sleep with my brother?'

Her expression tightened further, then loosened. 'Yes. Once.' The shark-smile settled back on her face. 'Will that be a problem?'

'Not necessarily.' If it was just the once, then probably not. If it was more than a one-off then whatever he knew, she probably did too. 'Do you know what the target of the job is?'

Not a waver in her expression this time. 'The financier behind this operation has been most insistent on confidentiality and discretion.'

Which didn't answer my question. I tried another tack. 'Did this individual approach you directly about the job? Or did you hear about it through Shiv?' I looked up at a slight sound, and the humming I'd almost tuned out stopped. The boy came in with a tea-tray. As he unloaded it I took a more thorough look around the room. It exhibited the characteristic Martian obsession with Feng Shui; I'd seen more Tara Mirrors, and breathed more flavours of incense in the last three days than in a year working at Everlight Europe. I put it down to spiritual over-compensation: bringing the familiar to an alien world. It was an odd juxtaposition with Ika's expensive and discreet comms equipment.

As the boy positioned the tea-pot – genuine china, or an impressive fake – Ika said, 'The blend is mainly Assam, so don't let it brew too long. Thank-you, Mani.'

When the boy closed the screen on his way out the hum re-started. I'd placed it while he was serving, as I'd been the one serving the tea during some delicate meetings back on Earth: Ika had jammers built into this room to stop eavesdropping, physical or electronic. She went up in my estimation.

Ika picked up a large but delicate-looking mug. She was having chai, from the smell of it. She blew on the drink, took a sip, then said, 'I have been honest with you. May I now expect the same courtesy in return?'

'Of course.'

'I was not aware Shiv had a sister, and after your call this morning I did a little research. Imagine my surprise to find you are an employee of Everlight, and have only recently arrived from Earth. Given this, I must ask: why are you here?'

I poured myself a cup of tea, and I took a sip. The leaves could have brewed a little longer, but it was a quality blend, and if that wasn't real milk it was an expensive substitute. Another point in this woman's favour.

Ika was still waiting for an answer.

'I don't know,' I admitted. Might as well have laid down on her sumptuous five-elements rug and bared my throat. 'I'm still thinking it through. You'd be within your rights to refuse to cooperate with me, under the circumstances.'

She nodded, and put down her mug. 'I have been trying to think what your agenda might be, what you might hope to achieve in coming here, and the most likely answer is that you want to take on the job.'

'Or to find out why my brother died.' That had been what I'd told myself when I called Ika to arrange our meeting.

'A noble motivation. It was a flyer accident, I believe.'

'And do you? Really believe that, I mean.'

'I have no idea. I don't go outside the domes if I can help it.'

'But you appreciate the sort of things that can go wrong, and the sort of people who can make them go wrong.'

'That's my job, but without knowing exactly what Shiv planned, I couldn't offer any meaningful suggestions.'

I could almost believe she hadn't known what Shiv was up to. Almost. 'If I did take this on it would require specialists. Shiv mentioned a couple but we'd have to recruit more.'

'I have made some initial approaches. Nothing has come of it, obviously.'

'Why not?'

'This was Shiv's job. He told me only what I needed to know.'

She was consistent, I'd say that for her. 'Ah, I got the impression you've had direct contact with the financier. So you don't know enough to take this on yourself?'

'The gentlemen in question made it clear he was looking for someone to lead in the field. In conducting my business, I never leave this room. I have suggested others who might coordinate the job but he appears to be looking for a certain type of person. If you think you might be that person then I would be willing, for a nominal fee, to put you in touch with him.'

'I can't pay you.'

'Hmm. You really have burnt your bridges, haven't you, Ms Choi?' She leaned in to toy with the handle of her chai mug. 'In the spirit of our continued honesty, I will say that I would very much like this job to be successful.'

'Even though you don't know what it is?'

'I knew Shiv, and liked him. More importantly, I know how much we can all make from this.'

'So it's in your interests to put me in touch with your man?'

She stared at the drink, and pursed her perfect lips. 'I will see what I can do.'

Even though Ika and I had danced round each other, I'd given more than I'd taken. She called the next morning, inviting me back to her parlour/office. 'I will leave you to take this call in private. You may rest assured that what passes between you will not be overheard.'

'Or recorded?'

'I have my reputation to think of.'

Which wasn't the same as saying 'No'.

I waited until the door was shut before acknowledging the flashing icon on her largest screen.

Ika had referred to the financier as 'he' but it was hard to tell from the image. Features blurred into a generic headshot; probably Caucasian and with a masculine hairstyle, but that was all I could tell. The background was a mash of muted brown and orange. Most likely the whole image was an artefact.

'Greetings, Ms Choi.'

The voice was low-register and probably male, though it was as modulated as the image was pixellated.

'Hello. What should I call you?'

'Whatever you like. Your brother called me Mr P, short for Mr Patron.'

Typical Shiv. 'Then that's what I'll do.' I found talking to this artefact disconcerting

'Good. I'll come straight to the point. What do you know about the job your brother took on for me?' I thought I could pick out a non-Chinese accent in his perfect, if distorted,

Mandarin. I'm good with languages.

'He planned to steal the Eye of Heaven.' It sounded absurd, saying it out loud. The largest, most valuable, most heavily guarded gemstone ever found.

'That's right. From your tone I'd guess you don't rate the success of this job.'

Of course, you can read my expression and voice, and I can't get a thing off you. Thanks for reminding me. 'Everlight's Martian HQ isn't going to be easy to penetrate.'

'No. But you're aware the Eye will be on public display in there?'

'I am. But only for the duration of the New Year celebrations.' Something Shiv had failed to mention. It put a time limit on the job. 'Even so, getting away with an opal the size of my head isn't going to be easy.'

'A lot of thought has already been put into this plan. I just need you to make it happen.' That accent. American? Irish? Australian? The latter was the most likely given that the Irish had zero presence on Mars – and he was on Mars, there was no signal lag – and America was history.

'You appear to be assuming I'll take on this job.'

'Not at all. If you're not interested, our contact ends here.'

'You need me to decide right now?'

'You've known what the job was for some time. You must have given your potential part in it plenty of thought.'

'I have.' As an abstract problem, a *What if?* To commit now, to tell this spooky stranger I was happy to break the law after a decade of obeying it ... 'If you make me answer now it'll have to be No. Sorry.'

'I'm sorry too.' The screen went dark.

Which left my other reason for being here: finding out what happened to Shiv. But there were only two explanations: either his death had been an accident, in which case there was nothing to find out, or it had been something more sinister, in which case if I, an outsider with no contacts or resources, started poking around, I was likely to have an 'accident' of my own.

My phone chirped as I stepped onto the walkway back to my hotel. A message from Mum. A recording rather than a call: being this far out had its advantages. Back in my new even smaller hotel room, I played it back.

'Beth, are you really on Mars?' She paused a moment, as though expecting me to miraculously break the light barrier with an answer. 'Shiv was planning something, you know. I think it was something big. Big, and special. On Mars. Where you are now, in fact.' She glanced to one side – she was in the same blue room – and grimaced. 'We owe it to your brother to find out what he was trying to do. You owe it to us, your family, to finish whatever he started. Ah, they're such misers; I have to go now. Stay safe, Elizabeth. Message me when you can.'

The recording ended.

Did she know what Shiv had been planning? I couldn't see how. No doubt they had enjoyed several cryptic conversations on well-monitored channels, and perhaps she even suspected this was the ultimate heist, the one she'd talked about taking on herself when we were younger… Just before she grew wings and flew into outer space. But she couldn't know for sure. Keeping tabs on me now Shiv was dead wouldn't be hard. I was her only living relative, after her short-sighted stupidity got my father, and everyone else in that hab, killed. Not that I'd known Wang-Zheng Choi well, given I'd been three years old when he tried to pay off this most inconvenient of mistresses, sending the three of us packing towards Earth. She couldn't even leave him honestly, and had only got as far as the LunaFree Community. That place had been the nearest I'd had to a home, for five years anyway, before she screwed them over too, and they threw us out.

The fact that my mother wanted me to take this job was reason enough not to.

But if I pulled it off I could pay to free her – thus removing any residual sense of obligation – and then pay to divorce her – thus removing her from my life.

I needed to take a step back.

Start by following the money. Ika was being well paid for her part in the potential theft of the Eye of Heaven. No doubt Shiv had been offered a generous fee as well. Who had the means to bankroll this type of job? An individual? Our 'Mr P' had said 'I', though that could be a ruse. There were some affluent loners on Mars, early investors who'd struck it rich and stayed on, but were any of them that rich? Hard to know, as those individuals valued their privacy, and living in private self-sufficient domes in an arid wilderness put you well out of circulation. It was possible someone with a lot of money and an eccentric love of valuable items was after the Eye, but I had no way of knowing who. I compiled a short-list anyway, with what little information was publically accessible. Interestingly, two of the individuals on my list gave their nationality as American: they had to be descended from early settlers who'd arrived here before their country went to radioactive hell after its idiotic experimentation in unlimited machine intelligence. Back in the twenty and twenty-first centuries the Americans had a reputation as uber-capitalists, collecting useless items just because they were considered valuable. According to the old movies and other popular media of the time, anyway.

Next I considered larger factions. Mars has a lot of factions but most of them are bit players, fighting for scraps from the Chinese table. Though now the Russians had recovered fully from the Marineris blowout they were a force to be reckoned with again. As were the Deimons, when it came to resources, at least: the Levi-Mathesons and their followers had been smart, far-sighted people who, once they'd hollowed out their moon and settled there permanently, had little use for the money that still flowed in from their many inventions and innovations. But their very lack of care for status or material wealth made them unlikely to want to steal a shiny rock whose only value was in the eye of the beholder.

Most likely it was a corp, one that opposed Everlight. Since one of their mining operations had come across the massive opal out in the Tharsis Ranges twenty years ago, the Eye of Heaven had become the heart of their Feng Shui web on Mars, the symbol and talisman of Everlight's inexorable rise to effectively rule the red planet. Stealing it would strike a blow beyond any that might be dealt via financial shenanigans or corporate politicking.

Ironically, the top contender in this scenario was none other than Four Flowers Holdings, my late father's employers. FFH were dominant on Luna but less of a player on Mars. Striking at Everlight in the domain where they held greatest power would be just the kind of spiritual coup they'd favour. Kind of ironic that I'd take a job working for FFH considering I had worked for them before, albeit briefly. My first attempt to go straight had involved using my father's influence – such as it had been – to get a job as a researcher and administrator with FFH NorthWest. And then Mum had reconciled with her old lover, and gone to live with him on Luna, where she poisoned him against me, their wayward and disrespectful daughter. She had also used her dubious connections to help him keep costs down on the new FFH hab. We all know how well that worked out. The worst week of my life occurred just over a decade ago when on three consecutive days I lost my job for reasons I could trace back to my parents but never contest, ended my latest attempt at a relationship, then heard the news about the hab explosion on Luna on a public com.

All of which was in the past, and such self-piteous navel-gazing wasn't getting me anywhere. Even so, the fact that I – and my brother before me – had been selected to take on this job was interesting. Not the FFH connection, now I thought about it – Shiv's father had been an Indian engineer and Wang had never formally adopted him – but the fact that we were both outsiders. Okay, so I'd only inherited the – potential – role, but our Mr P had been happy to consider me when, as Ika implied, he'd turned down local talent. This insistence on using outsiders both worried and intrigued me.

The next morning, when I went in search of the cheap sludge that passed for food around here, new red-and-gold decorations adorned the main walkways, and the open plaza near my hotel sported a wide scaffolding pillar reaching to the mezzanine above; at the base, half a dozen people in overalls were constructing something that looked like a giant claw out of spidersilk braiding and paper flowers. It was attracting some attention so I asked a passerby what was going on.

'They're building a lucky dragon,' the woman replied. She looked up at me appraisingly, registering my half-breed status. 'For the New Year, you know?'

Ah yes, New Year was less than a month away. I needed to get a move on.

I saw this movie once, a vintage piece from Japan. The newly-bereaved hero has a dream in which she dips her toe into a dark, inky lake, and the toe gets stained. When she wakes up, it's still stained. Over the next few days the stain rises up her body, turning her into living darkness. In the end, as it reaches her neck. She goes back to the lake and throws herself in, where she is reunited with her long-lost lover.

While I'd been dreaming, and rationalising, my toe had slipped into the water.

I called Ika. 'Can you contact the financier again, and ask if it's not too late?'

'I'm glad you've reconsidered Ms Choi.'

I smiled at the blurred image on Ika's screen. 'I didn't say that. I just said I'd like to talk.'

'Certainly. You have more questions, then?'

'One in particular. Why do you want an offworlder to run this job?

'Mars is a small and insular world. There are a limited number of people with suitable skills and although we'll have to use some local talent, I feel it's more likely to succeed if the individual coordinating the job, the only person with all the facts, is an outsider.'

Which was pretty much the answer I'd expected. My knowledge of the Martian underworld was limited but the Chinese dominated it, certainly in Olympus, Mars' first city, just as they did in mainstream Martian culture. A variation on the Triad system had been imported from Earth. I got the impression the relationship between the Triads and Everlight was complicated. I suspected that stealing Everlight's crown jewel was not something they'd be happy to attempt – or see anyone else attempt. I picked my next words carefully. 'Your original choice for this role suffered an unfortunate accident.'

'Yes. My condolences on your loss.' Of course he knew I was Shiv's sister; I'd have been more concerned if he hadn't.

'I haven't been able to find out much regarding that accident, other than the fact that it was a flyer crash, and the flyer apparently didn't have a working transponder. I don't suppose you know more than that?'

A momentary pause, then, 'You put me in a difficult position, Ms Choi. If we don't have a working relationship, I can't justify giving you that information. If we do, I'll share all I know, although some of it may... cause you concern.'

'So Shiv Neru's death wasn't an accident?'

'No one knows for sure.' Another pause. 'All right. I'll say this: there was evidence that an attempt had been made to capture the flyer.'

'Capture it? How?'

'Mars' low gravity combined with its minimal atmosphere means you can fly a small ground-launched vehicle into low orbit for relatively little power expenditure. You can even leave the gravity well entirely, if someone sends down a larger vehicle from orbit to snare your flyer before it reaches its operational limits.'

'Someone swooped down and snatched him out the sky before his flyer got to hard vacuum?'

'Not exactly. Most likely it was ambushed by a second vehicle in low orbit. The same structural mods that allow sub-orbital flyers to be snared also make them vulnerable to, well, hijacking.'

'Someone tried to *hijack* the flyer? It thought it crashed.'

'"Tried" is the relevant word. It is possible they wanted to capture Mr Neru, but something went wrong – perhaps he attempted to evade them – and the flyer was damaged, and crash-landed.'

My head was spinning. Shiv had always joked about never letting them take him alive. Looked as if it'd be his epitaph. But who were 'they'? Why did they want to capture him, out in the Martian wilderness? And what had he been doing taking a solo sub-orbital flight anyway?

'I think,' continued Mr P, 'that I've given you more than enough on trust.'

'Yes. You have.' Someone had tried to kidnap Shiv, and ended up killing him. Or killed him and made it look like a kidnap attempt. Was I letting myself in for similar treatment if I took on this job? I thought of my nice safe office job back on Earth; except it wasn't safe, and at best I'd get back to earning just enough to get by, and never find out what was going on here, or why my brother had got himself killed. Not to mention being guilt-tripped by my mother for the rest of my life.

'I'll do it.'

Four

Ika had already scoped out three members of the team, but I wanted to speak to them individually before hiring. I also asked her to get me a few prohibited items, for personal defence. Ika agreed though she commented, 'You do know Olympus Central is safer than most cities on Earth?' She might be right, given whoever had gone after Shiv had waited until he left the city, but I wasn't taking chances.

While Ika was arranging the interviews I received a message from my employers. Apparently my case was going through the formalities with Everlight's HR department, and after their initial ruling – expected in a few weeks, during which time I remained employed if unpaid – I would be expected to prepare a 'justification response'. I appreciated Mr Lau keeping me informed, but if everything worked out for me on Mars then Everlight HR could stick their initial ruling and request for justification in a place he'd be shocked to hear me refer to.

I chose neutral, public places for the interviews.

For the physical security expert I specified a mid-range tea-house. Xiao-Fei arrived on time and ordered green tea. He was a small man with a limp, and during the course of our conversation he used an inhaler twice. When I'd seen a Chinese name on Ika's file I'd been wary, and my wariness had increased on finding he had once worked for Everlight as an electrical engineer.

However, the blow-out at a remote dome which left him crippled had been hushed up, and the compensation he'd received barely covered his ongoing medical bills. He'd have no problem shafting his ex-employers.

Not that I told him he'd be doing that just yet. Our chat was suitably vague, an exchange of pleasantries, and some personal history from him (most of which I already knew, but I wanted to hear it from his own lips). Then I moved on to more detailed enquiries about the kinds of systems he was familiar with.

I was drawing on skills I'd gained in an office, rather than in my previous life aiding and abetting my mother; Mum preferred scams and schemes and the occasional hack, rather than open heists with accomplices. On those jobs where we'd brought in outside help she did usually tell them the target beforehand. But it's one thing hitting a local company or institution and quite another going up against the corporation who effectively rule the planet. Plus, the Eye of Heaven could be stowed out of our reach, back in Everlight's vaults, in a matter of minutes. I'd tell the team exactly what they were going after only when we were committed. Until then, I couldn't afford the slightest hint of a rumour to get out. As I say: compartmentalisation is vital in a job like this.

Speaking to my next contact meant returning to Ika's backroom data-fortress. This job required two hackers, with slightly different skillsets, in two different locations. Mr P had specified that the off-planet member of the team would be someone he'd recommend. Her name was Ana, and she insisted on a voice-only interview, which made getting to know her tricky, especially given her love of the local Martian patois, calling me *dost* and saying *shi* instead of *yes*. Most people I'd meet, correctly identifying me as an outsider, stuck to English or Mandarin rather than the mash-up of English, Mandarin, Russian and a variety of East Asian languages that all the cool kids spoke here. And she was a kid – she sounded appallingly young. I tried to see past the Martian dialect to identify her original accent; not mainland

Chinese, but somewhere around there. Taiwanese? Or even a Korean; there might be a few of them here, same as there were Americans. Perhaps she was on Phobos: the Pacific Rim Consortium, who ran that particular moon, enjoyed damaging Chinese interests. Or she was somewhere on one of the other stations above us. Maybe even a young and rebellious Deimon sticking it to the man. I just had to trust Mr P had picked wisely when he went for a teen in space.

Assuming she was what she sounded like. As I walked to the final meeting of the day, I considered the likelihood that Ana and possibly Mr P were not real people at all, but constructs voiced by a LAI. Then again, why use a Limited Artificial Intellect when I might suss I was talking to a machine? Just use masking software on a real human, as appeared to be the case here. And obviously they weren't Unlimited AIs. Not even the Deimons in their little bit of orbital semi-anarchy had managed – or perhaps dared – to recreate the perfect storm that led, briefly, to the only true AI. I doubted they'd be foolish enough to try, given how that worked out last time. But I was over-thinking this. All that mattered was that everyone played their part and the job went off smoothly.

The third team member who Ika had already vetted was Nico. His role fell somewhere between Xiao-Fei and Ana's, though he'd be working locally, on the ground. We met in one of the larger plazas, where drones flew delicacies from the nearby food court to diners' tables. Nico was there before me. We both ordered iced tea. He had mixed Malaysian and African heritage; he came across as laid-back and friendly, though his file said he was ex-military, an early experience as a conscript in southeast Asia he wasn't proud of. 'I'm here now, living a new life on Mars,' he said with a smile. My only concern was that he might have exaggerated his skills, as he struck me as a little too eager to please. Then again, much of his work would be done in advance of the job. Plus, I was looking for a mix of competencies hard to find in this environment and though I might have covered all the bases with two people taking on this role, I wanted to keep the numbers down.

The following day I met up with the final team member; our late addition, doing the job Shiv would have done, had he lived long enough.

The individual in question wished to be known as Gregori. He was Marineris-born and to go by the quality of the hotel he was staying at he wasn't in this for the money. I suspected Gregori was the rebellious playboy son of one of the old Russian families. I wondered at this, given the uneasy relations between China and Russia here and on Earth. But, though he was Martian-born, as a first-time visitor to Olympus he fulfilled Mr P's preference for using non-locals where possible, and nothing Ika managed to turn up gave us cause for suspicion.

We met in a coffee bar which, in the way of such offworld establishments, mainly sold over-priced coffee substitutes. He was late, which was a strike against him, and when he arrived he threw himself into the seat opposite me with a grin.

I tried to hold onto the fact that he was tardy, arrogant and might have dubious connections but mainly I tried to remember to breathe. He was in his early twenties, with sharp yet asymmetric features and immaculate blond hair. I have a thing for blonds. He'd look fantastic in Russian traditional costume, on the back of a black stallion. Were Cossacks blond? Who cared? He could ride across the steppes and pillage my village any time. *Yes, breathe.* I looked away from those lovely sapphire eyes and started the interview, only to have him interrupt as I was asking how long he'd been in Olympus.

'I get to drive and to pilot, yes?'

'Yes, you'll need both skills.'

'Good, good. Do you like to drive fast Ms C?' I'd taken a leaf out of Shiv's book and insisted my team used my title and first letter of my surname; hearing even part of my name from this young man made me feel a certain warmth. *Stay focused, and breathe.*

'We're not talking high performance vehicles here, Gregori.'

'No? But it'll still be fun.'

I managed to keep to my script for the rest of the interview. He flirted outrageously the whole time. I wasn't sure if this was an act for me or his default setting. Frankly, I didn't care.

I did ask one direct question I'd avoided with the others, it generally being considered bad form amongst career criminals. 'Why do you want to do this job?'

'Like I said, it'll be fun, da?'

I believed him. He really was that shallow. How charming. 'Let's hope so. I'm guessing, given where you're staying, the money is not the issue.'

'It is a good hotel. Spacious rooms.'

'Really? I'd be interested in seeing that for myself.'

'You like to see my room? I would love to show you.'

'Lead on.'

Two hundred or so years ago, back when humans first ventured into space, the idea of zero-gee sex used to be a Thing. It was meant to be exotic, special, out-of-this-world. Another example of how dumb our ancestors were. Leaving aside the chance that one or more partners would spend the session trying not to throw up, the laws of the universe do not bend just so a girl can get herself the right level of friction and degree of thrust to really hit the spot.

Low-gee sex with someone who knows what they're doing is, however, *a-maz-ing*. And Gregori knew what he was doing. Part of me wanted to stay all night – or what was left of it when I finally surfaced long enough to check the time – but that's not how I operate. Gregori, bless him, appeared genuinely surprised and sorry when I left.

Two days later myself, Nico and Gregori took a trip into the tunnels. Another key to success in a job like this, besides compartmentalisation, is diversion. Lifting the Eye was the simple part of the job; getting away with it would be the real challenge, and doing so without being caught was the reason we were being paid so much.

The final factor for any hands-on job is practice, although we were limited in what could be practiced in advance.

Ana, the team member with the fullest picture – including details on the target, so Mr P had better be right to trust her – would be doing whatever prep she needed on her own, high up in her orbital castle.

I was confident that Xiao-Fei knew how to deal with the on-site security we'd run into on the night. And before we went in I'd give him the full low-down on what was required, including the additional and rather unexpected part of the snatch.

Which left me, Nico and Gregori to run through the getaway, insofar as we could. We visited a part of Olympus most tourists avoided, the barely-used maze of first-generation tunnels dug by the original tunnelworms – the LAI-brained excavators invented by the Levi-Mathesons – along with so much we take for granted today, from spidersilk digesters to brain-deplaquing. Whatever I, or anyone else, might say about the LMs, they were the only non-corporate entity who got rich enough to buy a moon. And for all their high ideals, they kept their fortune by use of expedient cut-outs on their biotech which activate, rendering said tech useless, unless it gets regular catalytic boosts or similar tailored updates. These are sent out free from the Deimos labs… provided you'd paid the patent fees back to the founders' descendants.

Amusingly, the practice vehicles were rentals. Resources were limited here. All I could do was make sure they were as a close in spec as possible to the ones we'd be using on the night. This part of the run-through was more about getting familiar with the route than pulling fast stunts. You can't pull fast stunts in a tunnelbug. Not that this stopped Gregori trying. And though Nico was a competent driver, I needed a bit of practice. I'd driven various vehicles on Earth and Luna but my previous experience hadn't been underground. We ended up paying a damage excess on two of the 'bugs, thanks to Gregori's over-enthusiasm and my inexperience.

Halfway through our four days' of driving practice the Rainfall comet started final braking ready for insertion into Mars orbit. It looked unreal in the footage, a spiny black ball like some giant gothoid kid's toy. The black was the nanoweave coating, another LM special, necessary to keep the irregular ball of dirty snow intact until Everlight were ready to sell it off by the tonne. The news was cooing about this latest near-impossible feat by the corp. How had they managed it? A good question, but not one that bothered me much at the time.

By now we were only a week away from the start of the New Year celebrations, and Olympus' tunnels, plazas and shops were awash with red and gold décor and ingeniously constructed dragons ranging from the cute to the disturbing.

The day after Project Rainfall entered its penultimate phase I had an odd encounter. I was taking a narrow alleyway back to my doss-house – having seen inside Gregori's accommodation, I couldn't call it a hotel any more – when a man with an oversize backpack hurried out of a side turning. We ran into each other, and bundles of incense and lucky banknotes spewed from his backpack in Martian slo-mo. I reached out to help. Although the encounter had made me jump, he was old and bearded. Harmless. Probably. 'So very sorry,' he muttered as he pulled himself upright on me.

'No, no, it's my fault.' This kind of stunt could be a diversion, and I put my back against the slimy wall even as I helped the old man to his feet. Looking past him the alley appeared empty. 'Can you manage? Your stuff I mean?' This could still be a ploy, and I didn't want to get jumped while crouched down with hands full of ritual offerings.

'You hold my pack?'

I couldn't really refuse. I propped the pack against my leg, keeping my head up, while the old man gathered his gear up and re-packed it, fussing and muttering under his breath. As I lifted the pack onto his back he said, 'You like Olympus?'

'Er, yes. It's a great city.' He could guess I was a visitor; that was easy enough.

'So you stay for a while?'

'A while, yes.' I let go of the pack. He teetered for a moment, then turned to me. 'And you behave while you are here?' He actually waggled a bony finger at me.

I nodded. Not sure what else I could do.

He turned and bustled off.

Another film I remember, in fact I'm sure I've seen this trope more than once, is when the harmless old man who the stupid gwailo disregards later turns out to be the Grandfather of the local Triad family.

We couldn't practice with the second vehicle we'd be using. We were in the hands of Mr P and Ana for that part of the job. All we could do was make sure we got to it safely.

External airlocks aren't remote hackable any more – humans learnt by that mistake in the Selene City disaster. You have to be physically present to deal with them. Hacking one in situ is possible, but if you're in a hurry, or you don't have the skills, you need something a little more... primitive.

And that was how the three of us came to take another rented vehicle, this one a rover rather than a tunnelbug, on a day-trip to the outside slopes of Olympus Mons itself.

Given what had happened to my brother, I went armed with the most impressive weapon Ika had procured, an ancient-looking concussion pistol, firing actual slugs. Not at all legal, so I couldn't wear it openly in the domes. It wouldn't be wise to let off a shot in the rover either, but I felt better knowing I had a weapon to hand. Once we were outside the city proper, I strapped the holster on my belt. Nico gave me a dark look, but said nothing. Gregori raised his eyebrows at the chunky sidearm, before smiling and commenting that he found girls with big guns very sexy. *Breathe, and focus, Lizzie. Breathe and focus.* I kept both my accomplices in sight as far as possible. That way, if one of them tried anything, the other might, hopefully, intervene.

It took most of the day to reach the target area, as we were practising on long-disused and semi-depressurized tunnels far enough away from any habitation that our activities would remain undetected. We also had limited materials for this dry run, as we had to save enough for the job itself.

It took Nico half an hour to do this stuff out at the chosen airlock. Gregori and I had nothing to do but wait, back in the rover. This vehicle, being somewhat more expensive than the tunnelbugs, had internal cameras, one covering the cab, one looking out, so we'd parked facing downslope with a panoramic view of red rubble sweeping down towards the distant plains below. If it wasn't for the clause saying we'd lose our deposit on the rental if we took our skinsuits off, Gregori and I might have given anyone who reviewed the internal footage something interesting to watch.

The time ticked by. If Gregori wasn't the vacuous and cute creature he appeared to be then now, with Nico out of sight, would be the time to make his move. The camera coverage wasn't perfect; a gun drawn behind the pilot's seat, pointed forward, might not even be recorded. And cameras could be tampered with.

I told myself that these paranoid fantasies weren't helping and indulged in some more healthy, if filthy, ones. Given he hadn't shot me, I'd be going back to Gregori's when we were done here.

Finally Nico commed, summoning us out to witness his handiwork. We donned breathers and went outside. This was the first time I'd stood on the unprotected surface of another planet, and I tried to savour the experience, but it was a lot like a technicolour version of the Moon, though with splashes of sulphur and grey hardy-lichen on some of the sunnier rocks. Nico had found one such rock, which he now suggested we stayed behind, 'just in case'. This did not reassure me.

The charge was on a timer, but being monitored from his suit. He counted it down over the comm, as a courtesy. 'Three... two... one.'

The ground kicked. A plume of rock, dust and bits of metal airlock spurted out the side of the mountain. A lot more rock, dust and metal than I'd expected. Despite the thin air, the accompanying bang was loud enough to hurt the ears. If anyone was listening in Olympus, they'd have heard that.

I took a deep breath to calm myself, then turned to Nico.

'You're only supposed to blow the *outer* airlock!'

Nico smiled, and shrugged apologetically. Behind him, debris began to rain down on the Martian landscape.

When we got back to the domes, I half expected Nico's over-enthusiasm to have got us in trouble. The tunnel he'd breached had been sealed further in so we hadn't caused a blow-out, but an explosion that size could register on seismic sensors and as Mars wasn't prone to earthquakes that could have raised questions. When no one asked about our little trip I concluded we'd been far enough out that no one had noticed.

But that evening did bring some bad news. Ika called to say Xiao-Fei had been arrested.

'What for?' I demanded.

'My sources didn't say. We have no reason to suspect it relates to the current endeavour.'

No reason to assume it didn't, either. I had a sudden urge to check escape routes. My options for leaving Mars were limited, not least by lack of funds. If I wanted to use my budget return I'd need to wait a week.

Late morning the next day the news got worse. Xiao-Fei had suffered an 'incident' while in police custody, and was now in a coma. His health hadn't been good and it might just be that, an accident, maybe even a reaction to stress. Or he might have been interrogated, with prejudice. I hated myself for hoping he was just ill, as opposed to a victim of police brutality, but he was in no position to have an opinion right now.

Two flights left before New Year, one to Phobos (affordable) and one back to Earth (not). Or I could head out to Marineris, let Gregori show me the sights there. Then again, if Xiao-Fei *had* squealed, they'd be watching the ports. Or I could call off the job, leaving me broke and in bad favour with Ika and our patron. But also alive, and out of prison. Perhaps I should hope for bad weather, as that would scupper the job without pissing anyone off. Act of God, and all that. But the forecast was for a fine and dust-free New Year.

I'd got to know a few locals around my doss-house over the last couple of weeks. Relationships varied from polite but distant through to the kind of street camaraderie I sometimes found growing up with Mum and Shiv; in order to end up here I must've had at least as crappy a time as they had, and that made me okay. One of the friendlier locals, an ever-cheerful sex worker of variable gender called Wu, asked if I'd heard about old Mr Feng.

'Not sure I know who you mean.' The street camaraderie came with an assumption that you knew what they knew, but I'd hadn't had much chance to get a feel for the neighbourhood.

Wu waved a rainbow-nailed hand. 'Had a fall, and he's in the Charity. Such a miser, he wasn't poor you know, he could have afforded a trolley, or hired help, but no, he had carry his business on his back.'

'In a backpack?'

'Yes! So you do know him. Silly old coot.'

Some coincidences are just that: coincidences. Not enemy action. And some harmless old men really are harmless old men, not venerable crime-lords. Being cautious to the point of paranoid compulsion can be counter-productive.

I called Ika, and asked if she could get hold of anyone with Xiao-Fei's skillset in the time we had left.

Her name was Paula McIntyre and she was a genuine American. We met at a different tea-house to the one where I'd spoken to Xiao-Fei. Give how tight the schedule was, I considered not meeting her at all, but everyone else had been interviewed and if this last-minute replacement for Xiao-Fei didn't pan out, the job wasn't happening.

She was older than any of us, mid sixties at least, with an easy-going smile and a gaze that didn't miss a trick. She'd only arrived in Olympus recently, from Earth, and her profession was openly listed as 'security consultant'. As with the others, our chat was mainly small talk. When I commented on her strong US accent she said, 'My parents saw the Small War.'

'Saw as in...' She was old enough to only be one generation removed from the worst thing humanity had ever done to itself, but I had trouble getting my head around how you can 'see' a nuclear exchange that sterilised half a continent, and survive.

'They were hiking in the Rocky Mountains when it went down. Kinda ironic, really.'

'Because that's where the Doomsday UAI was?' It was still a chilling thought, the idea that an inhuman intelligence could decide it made sense to wipe out a whole nation just because they were the enemy de jour. To this day, no one was quite sure how that disastrous first strike had come about.

'Yeah. Pop said they had no idea what was going on until they saw a mushroom cloud on the horizon. Then he checked his cell and when there wasn't any coverage, assumed the worst.'

'But the fallout...' She didn't look like the mutant child of irradiated parents.

'They were in the far north, and the wind was blowing from that direction. They walked across the Canadian border about the same time the Generals took an axe to that damn AI.' She sounded angry about it, even though she hadn't been born then.

Despite myself, I liked this woman. I felt a little star struck – because the only thing rarer than a genuine full-blood American is a genuine full-blood North Korean – but there was also an unexpected sense of kinship. Mum played up her quarter-heritage US blood, so I watched a lot of old US movies when I was growing up. Paula McIntyre was the 'real deal'. For a moment I wanted to take her into my confidence, tell her up front what the target was. But much as I enjoyed talking to her, I'm the daughter of a con-artist. I don't trust that easily.

Twelve hours later, we were crawling through ducts together. Having two people go in to physically lift the Eye was risky, but Mr P wanted me present for the whole job. 'You can't be sure what you'll find; you might need two people for some of it. And you're the person on the ground I hired, so you're the only one I want handling the Eye.'

With Mr P's words ringing in my ears, I still hadn't told Ms McIntyre what we were here to steal. All she knew was that the target was somewhere in Everlight's main corporate complex – that being where we were now. She didn't look happy when I told her she'd get full details in due course but she was also a professional, and she didn't gripe.

'Which way here?' She was in front, and we'd come to an intersection.

'Left,' I muttered into my comm. Her coverall-clad backside got moving again. We'd dressed as maintenance workers, a basic disguise which, along with some remote hacking from Nico, had got us into the ducts.

'Okay.' We crawled forward. Just round the corner, she stopped. 'Hold up, we've got a sensor grid here.' We both wore hudglasses; mine projected a map, while hers showed an overlay of radiant energy, temperature fluctuations, the UV and IR spectrum and other arcane environmental factors that could alert someone who knew what to look for to hidden security features.

'Right. Time to do your stuff, Paula.'

Ducts feature in a certain type of US film. They're great plot devices but lousy design choices. I mean, why would you build a secret entrance into your secure facility? On Mars, where you need to circulate a manufactured atmosphere to a lot of people living in sealed, confined spaces, you really do need some person-sized ducts. But whilst these ducts had got us into Everlight's territory, the sensitive areas weren't accessible this way. And, being Everlight, they'd built security features into some of these low-security ducts. In this case, a lattice of invisible laser beams that triggered an alarm if anything larger than a rat passed through; or if someone tried to disarm them and failed. I'd hoped we might get the locations of these little surprises from Nico's preliminary research, but he'd said he couldn't risk going that deep into Everlight's security system, so we were on our own.

I sat back and counted breaths. I'm not phobic about confined spaces, but I am afraid of being caught. This was the first obstacle we'd come across requiring Ms McIntyre's skill. She'd better be up to it.

Sixty-seven breaths later she said, 'We're clear.'

We set off again. My breathing remained shallow until I was sure we'd passed the unseen detection device. Logically, I should have continued to worry: if we had tripped an alarm it was probably silent. We could handle one possible response to Everlight discovering our route in; if they were irresponsible enough to pump knock-out gas into their own vents, we had rebreathers. More likely they'd just station guards at the exits. It'd be a while before we found out.

'It would be good to know where we're heading, Ms C.'

Maybe it was time to show a little trust. 'I'll ping you the map.'

'Thanks.' We crawled a few more metres. 'The Celestial Colonnades?'

'That's right.'

'Ah.' That, to use the US parlance, was the sound a woman doing the math. Her next comment confirmed it. 'That's where the Eye of Heaven is currently on display.'

I could have dissembled, pointed out how many other

expensive artefacts and trophy objects Everlight must have in their corporate museum, but I'd decided to trust her. 'Yep.'

'Ah.' And that was the sound of a woman considering consequences. Maybe she'd suspected we were after the Eye, but now she knew. If she wasn't kosher, if she had another agenda, this might be the moment she made her move. Then again, her current position, on hands and knees in front of me in a narrow crawlspace, wasn't the place for it. 'Thanks for letting me know.'

I got nothing from her neutral tone: not gratitude, not sarcasm, not concern.

We carried on.

Two corners later she found another detection device, this one pressure-based. It took a long time to disarm. If Everlight were mustering the troops, they'd be in place by now.

Round the next corner, our duct ended in a grill. My mouth dried up. We were about to break cover.

'Anyone out there?' I murmured over the comm.

'All clear.'

'Good. I'm assuming you can get that grill off safely?'

'Shouldn't be a problem.'

It wasn't; from the speed she dealt with it I suspected the grill hadn't even been alarmed. As Paula pulled it free of its frame she asked, 'Are we coming back out this way?'

'Nope.'

'Good.' She probably didn't fancy making a quick getaway on hands and knees. Me neither.

Before we left the ducts we wriggled out of our coveralls. Underneath we wore skinsuits provided by Mr P which, when we pulled the hoods up, would mask body heat (except for our exposed faces) block scents and pheromones (not really an issue unless they had some very quirky security) and (the thing we were most likely to need in here) provide a basic chameleon function.

Unfortunately, this high-tech bonus was rather offset by the need to keep our low-tech coveralls with us. The bodysuits should have stopped us getting any DNA traces on the coveralls, and Shiv might have assumed they had and left them stuffed in the ducts, but I don't take chances. We bundled the coveralls into our expandable backpacks, which were also camo'd up.

Paula eased the grill back into place after we'd climbed out. Having Everlight think we'd left that way might be useful if we triggered any defences, but we couldn't leave any traces while we were still in the building.

We were in a carpeted corridor with anaemic yellow walls relieved by the occasional abstract print in pinks and reds. Executive country, Mum would call this. I'd spent much of the last decade passing through similar corridors, though not as an intruder.

We both had the map and there was room to walk side-by-side, so we did. Two things could scupper us before we reached the target area: surveillance and foot patrols. For the former, we had to rely on Nico's worm to ensure any cameras or other sensors along our path fed back nothing but empty corridor. Assuming his hack hadn't been detected. For foot patrols, we had to rely on our wits. Or, if it came to it, on the stunguns we both carried.

Worst case would be running into guards who either saw us first and raised the alarm, or who we dealt with only to have their colleagues back at base wonder why their mates suddenly disappeared off the security feed. Nico should be was busy setting up the next part of the plan by now, with neither the connectivity nor the time to monitor the local security feed and give us a heads-up of incoming trouble.

It wasn't far to the Celestial Colonnades. We took it slowly, pausing at the two intersections we passed. No sound save the faint hum of aircon. No smell save the faintest whiff of the most expensive incense.

Our destination wasn't hard to find. Amongst plain doors only identified by discreet pseudo-metal panels an actual metal door, standing floor-to-ceiling, stood out. Up closer and it was clear this was two bronze doors, decorated with a bas-relief design of dragons and clouds, like something from an ancient feudal castle. There was no obvious handle.

Paula McIntyre stood in front of the doors and pursed her lips. Finally she said, 'This looks interesting.'

'But not impossible.'

'Oh no. I love a challenge.'

I didn't tell her to shelve relishing the challenge in favour of getting on with the job. She knew that. Instead I said, 'I'll keep watch,' and padded up to the nearest junction. Glancing back, I saw her swing her pack round and remove several small objects. I recognised the flat palm-sized square of a sequencer, and a clear-cased micro-tool kit. I left her to it, and looked away, focusing on the intersecting corridor.

I'd been involved in two physical heists in my youth. One was an art heist in St Petersburg where I'd been a surprisingly lo-tech spotter; I'd been fourteen at the time. Two years earlier I'd had my only other experience in the ducts, when Mum had realised that the Cairo Museum had service tunnels a child could fit through. Those jobs had ended in success, though only just in St Petersburg.

However, in both cases we'd checked out the location in advance. That hadn't been an option here. Though Everlight liked to show off their prized possessions, most of the time access was limited to those they thought deserved it, which generally meant the execs of other corps. Over the New Year they also let the great unwashed visit the company showcase, but only in the most regulated way. You applied for tickets – which were expensive, and required personal vetting to even request – and a lucky few hundred would get guided tours of the company's spiritual heart at this most propitious of seasons. Obviously, I hadn't applied. So, other than knowing the general shape of the rooms beyond that door, I was going in blind.

It could have been worse: outside New Year the Eye was sealed in secure storage, in an unknown location in the complex.

Movement! Two guards were sauntering down the corridor. I

withdrew my head and hissed a warning to Paula. 'Fight or flight?' she asked over the comm.

'Neither. Hide. But keep your gun to hand.' I'd already drawn mine, and was jogging back towards the double doors. Once I saw Paula had her stungun out and was turning to face the wall I did the same, opposite her but a little offset, the hand with the gun in pressed into the wall, hidden by my skinsuit camouflaged body. If the guards spotted an odd bit of wall as they approached then we'd both turn and fight, catching them in the crossfire. Where were Paula's tools? She wouldn't have had time to gather them up, so they'd be on the floor near her feet, visible to anyone who looked. Should we just fire on the guards as soon as they reached the junction? I wasn't sure how we'd know when that was, or how effective we'd be. I don't carry lethal firearms on a job but stunguns aren't the best range weapons.

I heard voices. The guards, a man and a woman, were griping about missing a New Year's party. Good. If they were talking they weren't watching their surroundings. Plus, we'd know where they were. I made myself breathe slow and even.

Their voices got suddenly louder. '...not as though the overtime rate even makes it worthwhile...'

Then quieter.

I took a proper breath. They'd walked straight past the end of the corridor. They hadn't even looked our way. Holiday cover staff: never the sharpest.

'Close call,' murmured Paula in my ear as she unpeeled herself from the wall.

'Let's hope it's the only one.'

Another good thing about the skinsuit is that it absorbs sweat. My body was reminding me how far I was out of my comfort zone. I respected Mr P's logic, but I'd still rather not be here. Given the choice, I'm an organiser not a cat-burglar.

I jumped at Paula's voice in my ear. 'We're in.'

One of the great doors clicked open. I went over and peered inside. I smelt old incense on the air, but saw nothing except darkness in the room beyond. As I switched my hudglasses to lo-light mode Paula nodded into the dark room and asked, 'We sure the lights aren't on auto?' A reasonable question, especially if tripping said lights showed up on someone's status board.

'Not according to the schematics we've got.' Schematics which hadn't shown the security measures in the ducts. I hate unknown unknowns.

I gestured for Paula to go first. She shot me a look which I couldn't make much of through her now-opaque glasses, and stepped across the threshold.

Nothing happened.

I followed her.

'Let's close this,' I said, nodding back at the metal door once we were both in the room.

'Good idea.'

It took both of us to pull the door closed manually, using the handle on the inside. I didn't like the solid *thunk* it made when it swung back into place but we couldn't risk any guards who were paying attention finding it open.

The plans showed four large, square rooms, each one big enough to swallow my old apartment. I had no information about the internal layout but we appeared to have stepped into history. We stood under an arch leading into a courtyard formed by tiled, ridged roofs reaching down on all four sides. I glanced up, half expecting to see stars, but there was just the high ceiling. No doubt the lighting, when it was on, included suitably atmospheric projections.

The courtyard was full of artfully arranged statues. Lion-dogs, dragons, nymphs, and, in pride of place in the centre, a life-sized Buddha in the Tibetan style. It was hard to tell in this – lack of – light, but the Buddha appeared to be carved from a single lump of solid jade. Some of the statues looked new; others so ancient and weathered I wasn't even sure what they'd once been. Of course, nothing here was genuine, hauled up Earth's gravity well and shipped all the way to Mars. But they would be faultless reproductions of items Everlight did own.

I was reasonably sure we wouldn't find the Eye in this room, but we had to check. 'I'll go left, you take the right,' I said to Paula.

'Sure.'

As I picked my way through the statues I heard a gentle murmur from up ahead. After a moment, I identified it as running water. Other than the statues the only other features were the stone benches against the walls; the walls themselves were painted with detailed murals of Chinese myths and legends.

We met up on the threshold of the next room. 'Do you want me to go first this time?' I asked Paula.

'Whatever works for you.'

'Let's do this together then.'

We entered side-by-side to find ourselves in another courtyard, though this time containing a sculpted garden, complete with stream running diagonally across the middle. As well as the benches around the edge there were love-seats and carved arbours amongst the well-trimmed hedges and gravel paths. The only way across the stream was a delicately curved metal bridge. Paula went first. Halfway across, movement from below caught my eye. I froze. There was something in the water, something big. A fish. Of course. Not just any fish: a carp as long as my arm, beautifully mottled. Probably cost what I used to earn in a year.

The next room had a number of large square objects in it, some of them reflecting what little light came from behind us.

'Wait!'

I froze at Paula's whisper. 'What is it?'

'I think we've got a pressure-pad here.' The woman was certainly earning her share. She came up to stand next to me, then crouched down and reached out in a sweeping motion, hand just above the patch of floor between the two rooms, where the gravel of the garden gave way to polished stone. 'Yeah, it's inbuilt and passive.'

'Can you deal with it?'

'Not easily. Like I said, inbuilt and passive.'

'Ah. Yes.' Sensors like this were part of a structure's fabric, in this case probably a property of the pseudo-stone in front of us. You couldn't turn them off without removing the floor. Most of the time, the signal they sent wouldn't trigger an alarm – as otherwise every visitor to the place would be tripping its security – but they'd be switched to 'live' mode whenever the Colonnades were locked up. 'What do you reckon your chances of dealing with it are?'

'Fifty-fifty at best. And it'll take some time.'

I respected her honesty. We were on a schedule. I looked up, as though there might be some convenient hand-holds on the ceiling. There weren't. I looked down again, beyond her to the floor of the next room. It was lacquered wood; the stone only covered the area under the carved archway between the two rooms, about two meters in total. 'How likely is it the sensors extend beyond the area of stone flooring?'

'Highly unlikely.'

'Then how about we just jump over it?' In this gravity, two metres was nothing.

'I... guess we could. Yes, that would work.'

We backed up as far as the topiary would allow. 'I'll go first,' I said. I sprang forward, my feet pounding gravel. The sudden physical exertion felt odd, an explosive relief. I pushed off, was in the air for a long moment, then landed, well into the other room. As I stepped back to let Paula take her jump I wondered how poor Xiao-Fei would have dealt with this obstacle.

Paula landed a little behind me, though still clear of the stone floor.

This room was full of glass cases. The cases contained what could only be described as military memorabilia. Swords, pikes, suits of armour and, as a centrepiece, a replica horse and rider, all clad in scale mail which, in normal light, probably shone bright as gold. Like everything else seen through the hudglasses, the place appeared to be lit by strong moonlight. In the first two rooms with their outdoor artifice, this had been apt, even relaxing, but here, amongst all the gleaming weaponry and glass, the effect was disconcerting. We checked the cases methodically. I found one sword which claimed to be the genuine article, imported all the way from Szechuan by a named executive I'd never heard of to celebrate his promotion; by implication everything else was a replica, as I'd assumed. The Eye wasn't here.

I paused on the threshold of the final room until Paula had done her checks. All clear.

This last room also contained glass cases, plus some free-standing exhibits. Rather than martial treasures, here we had jewellery, fabric, pots and incense burners. The free-standing figures – which looked disturbingly lifelike through my hudglasses, save for their blank eyes – were dressed in silk costumes straight out of the old Imperial Court.

No immediate sign of what we were here for, though. We worked our way back. And there, against the back wall, was the Eye of Heaven. Sitting in its black cradle on a black plinth, it was easily the brightest thing in the room. Even in the lo-light the Eye shone like a giant pearl coated in rainbows. It wasn't quite a perfect oval, being more egg-shaped, like something you might expect a phoenix or other mythical creature to hatch from.

Paula came to stand next to me.

The other exhibits were close-packed, but the Eye had its own distinct space, with nothing save air for a metre on each side. Which could just be part of the whole Feng Shui effect, giving it the room to do its spiritual stuff. Or it could indicate invisible security measures. 'That's a suspiciously empty bit of room they've chosen,' I remarked

'Sure is. I'll check it out.' Paula knelt and extracted her equipment from her backpack. I stepped back to give her space. I'd come up with a provisional schedule for the job, though I'd had to built in plenty of contingency, given our incomplete intel. By the timings I was using as a baseline, we were running seventeen minutes late. I reminded myself that it was just that, a baseline; not a deadline. There was leeway built in.

Paula finished running a hand-held detector over an area of wall at the right-hand edge of the Eye's exclusion zone, and returned to her stash of gear. She selected what looked like a shiny cosmetic compact, laid it flat on her palm and opened it sideways, like a little hardcopy book. She turned away from the Eye and flicked her wrists. The mirrored 'book' extended out to a metre-long conduit, two slivers of mirror connected at a ninety-degree angle to each other, foil-thin but rigid.

I'd seen reflectors like this before. They took a lot of skill to deploy, and they only worked on certain types of light-grid. I had to assume Paula knew this was such a grid. She stood the reflector on the floor. I stepped back. The bottom edge had nano-grip technology, but it would still teeter if knocked. Next, Paula fitted a pair of black rods, so slender they were barely visible, across the top and, after reversing it, the bottom of her mirrored conduit. With the rods in place, she picked up the reflector, and spent a while just looking at the Eye and its surrounds. Then she edged forward. She stopped, and adjusted her grip to hold the reflector's base just off the floor. Moving so slowly she appeared not to be in motion at all, her face blank with concentration, she extended her arms.

I realised it had been some time since I'd taken a breath, but my chest was too tight to let much air in.

Paula lowered the reflector the final couple of millimetres to the floor. Her shoulders lowered by about the same amount.

Stage one complete. Now the tricky bit.

She crouched down then turned her head, checking the (to me) invisible beams. I could have reset my hud display too, but seeing what Paula was seeing wouldn't make me any less nervous. I had to trust her to do her job.

Placing one hand on the thin connector rod running across the top of the reflector, she began to move her fingers apart. Her other hand was still half extended, not quite touching the reflector, like a magician in the middle of a conjuring trick.

The two halves of the reflector began to slide apart. Now they were connected only by the expanding rods at top and bottom.

Would the alarm be silent, if she tripped it? I had an idea not, at this stage. My ears hurt from waiting for the klaxon.

The gap widened. Now the two slivers of mirror had clear air between them – clear of any sort of detecting light beam, that is. If I was only ten centimetres wide I could slip in there right now.

The gap widened further. There was a trade-off here: the bigger the gap, the easier it would be to get through, but the farther apart the two halves of the reflector got, the less stable they were, even with their nanotech footing. I consoled myself that this was probably easier in Martian gravity before remembering that Paula came from Earth. Was she assuming one G, not a third? Should I point this out? I opened my mouth, then closed it again. She didn't need me whispering in her ear unexpectedly.

The gap was a good forty centimetres now. Paula kept teasing out the upper supporting rod, which was slaved to the lower one. I saw a ripple of tension in her thigh, the muscles protesting at being held in a tense squat for so long. *Perhaps we should have brought a folding stool.*

If the alarm was silent, the guards would be here any moment.

She stopped, with the gap at what my hudglasses told me was fifty-two centimetres. She stood and pummelled her aching legs – but gently, so as not to disturb the reflector. With it set this wide, fierce aircon might sway it and it only took a tiny movement to misalign the beams currently being reflected back to their source in the wall. At which point, we'd be blown.

'We good?' I whispered. Then I made myself take a proper breath.

'We're good.'

She looked past her handiwork to the plinth with the Eye on

it. 'No case. That because of the Feng Shui energies?'

'Most likely.'

'The plinth'll be rigged. Won't know how until I get in there.'

'Anything I can do?'

'Stay back unless I say otherwise.'

'Got you.'

Despite the tension, I did relish seeing a master at work.

Paula gathered a subset of tools into her backpack and slung it round her neck, facing forward. Then she crouched down and sidled sideways towards the gap between the two halves of the reflector.

Part of me wanted to watch, but that part stopped me breathing. I looked away, because this was the messy human bit of the job, where a slip or a sneeze could mean disaster.

When I looked again, Paula was straightening on the other side of the invisible doorway. She approached the Eye with all the care I'd expect, taking readings, holding out a palm, cocking her head.

'I reckon we've got a basic pressure-trap here.' Her voice was all business.

'You reckon? You can't be sure?'

'Not without touching it, and I want to have everything prepped before I do.'

'But you can deal with whatever you do find?' We were thirty-two minutes behind schedule now.

'Yes and no. Fooling the weight-sensor shouldn't be an issue but this is a no-expense-spared set-up, so it's likely to have spatial sensors too.'

'Meaning?'

'When I lift the Eye from its cradle, we'll need to replace it with something as near as possible the same shape. Some of those pots back there—'

'Actually,' I said, 'We need to take the cradle too.' I should have mentioned that earlier. Bad Lizzie.

Her head swung round, though her face was blank behind

her hud. 'What?'

'That octagonal holder it's sitting in? We can't lift the Eye from it.'

'Can't as in…'

'I've been instructed to bring the Eye of Heaven out in its holder.'

'Do we know why?' Her voice was cold.

'Because those are our instructions.'

She nodded, and said nothing. Then finally, 'You're the boss.' She turned away and resumed her observations and calculations. A minute and a half later she said. 'Actually that'll make it easier. I'm picking up some odd environmental readings but no obvious security on the plinth itself.'

'Good. And you'll monitor those odd readings?'

'Of course.'

She stepped closer, and touched the plinth. No alarm sounded. She shucked off her backpack and selected the micro-tool kit, then bent over the plinth. After less than a minute she straightened, put a hand on either side of the Eye, then lifted it free, cradle and all. I savoured the lack of obvious alarms.

'Hhhmm.' She sounded disappointed.

'Problem?'

'No. Opposite in fact. The cradle was just screwed into the plinth. No security on it at all. Perhaps our patron knew something about the Eye's holder, and decided it was beyond anyone's skill to deal with it.' She appeared to take this as an affront to her skills.

'That could be it.' Not that I had any more idea than she did why Mr P wanted the Eye of Heaven in its not-at-all-handy carrying cradle. I'd had to accept this as one of his quirks. He was paying, after all.

I wondered if Paula would just hand me the Eye but she stuffed it into her backpack and slung it across her front.

'Are you going to be okay like that?' The Eye wasn't quite head-sized, but it had to be heavy. It would pull her off balance when she did her crab-through-a-crevice routine.

She just grunted. It wasn't like I could intervene.

It was even harder to look away this time, but I needed to let her concentrate. When I heard a small gasp I screwed my eyes shut, like that would help. When I opened them she was frozen in place between the two halves of the reflector, both hands on the floor, pack swinging dangerously free. She'd fallen forward, then caught herself.

'Can I –?'

'No. I'm good.' She leant back, getting her weight redistributed. Then she shuffled out from between the two reflector posts. Once she was sure she was clear, she stood, and eased her neck from side-to-side.

I waited until she had ironed out the kinks before saying, 'I'll take the Eye now please.'

'Why?' Her hud was still opaque, but I suspected she was looking askance.

'It's nothing personal. Just another of the patron's conditions.'

'And the patron will know we obeyed this particular request how?'

'Look, I know it's a pain, but let's do this by the book.'

'Whatever.'

Time was ticking. 'Let's just swap packs.'

'Sure.' She sounded tense.

Getting Paula's now-heavy pack on my back proved tricky. When she offered to help I didn't object. What can I say, I was tired and stressed and in a hurry. Standing behind me, she supported the pack while I threaded my arms through the straps. As I shrugged the pack onto my shoulders I felt her step away to the side.

Something stung my cheek, a needle-prick of cold. I went to swat at what I assumed must be a biting insect. Reality dawned somewhere between brain and hand.

Paula McIntyre had just shot me.

The stunguns Ika had procured for us were fast-acting and, pissed off though I was, I was still conscious. It had been Ika's idea to give our newest team member untipped darts 'just in case'. If we'd had to deal with security guards that would put us at a disadvantage, but weighing up the odds of getting into a fire-fight versus a potential double-cross from the lovely Paula, I'd concurred with the fixer.

I drew my own pistol from its waist holster and stepped back, keeping the reflector in the corner of my eye. Tripping over that would not improve my situation.

Paula was giving her gun an incredulous stare. She didn't look happy. Her resume hadn't mentioned combat skills. I hoped it had been accurate.

She shot again. Our skinsuits would protect against a stun dart so her target was small, just the unprotected lower half of my face. She missed.

My target was equally hard to hit, being the lower half of *her* face. But I had to take her down quickly.

Mum hadn't been big on combat skills, but Ahmed, the boyfriend she'd kicked around with during our year in Afghanistan, had been all for training me up because, he said, 'girls are often at a disadvantage'. I'd been thirteen at the time, and full of fury at the world. I'd paid attention during his lessons.

Instead of cracking off a wild shot I stepped backwards, once, twice, keeping my eyes on the target and the gun raised, taking aim even as I put distance between us. I couldn't risk more than two steps back thanks to the forest of display cases, and the fact that, having shot again, she was now closing on me, her face full of angry desperation.

Now or never. I fired.

No recoil, unlike some of the weapons Ahmed had put in my hands. I missed: she kept coming.

I stepped back again, and banged my heel on something solid. I fired through a flash of pain from my bruised heel.

She was at lunging distance now. She lunged.

The lunge became a fall, her eyes defocusing as the drug kicked in. Thanks to the display case I'd backed up against, I ended up catching her in my arms. Her anger had drained away, under the influence of industrial-strength sedation and, perhaps, acceptance of the inevitable.

As I lowered her to the floor her gaze sharpened and she smiled. Her eyes fluttered closed, but just before she went limp she murmured, 'Mr Lau sends his regards.'

Five

What the hell was I supposed to do now?

Stick to the plan, that was what.

I could work out what Paula meant later. Right now, I had to get out of here.

I had the Eye, and the lack of guards, alarms or security lights suggested that, despite Paula McIntyre's duplicity, the job was still on. I shifted my pack more firmly into place, and left my traitorous accomplice to her drugged sleep. By the time I was through the first room I was all but running. Jumping the pressure-pad in the doorway between the armoury and garden rooms felt like flying. Then I landed, and the Eye shifted on my back. I stumbled, then caught myself. I was pumped, more alive than I'd been for a decade. And that was dangerous. I made myself walk across the garden and through the statues.

When I reached the door, I pulled at the handle. Nothing. Not pull: *push*. I pushed. It didn't move. I was locked in.

No: think, Lizzie. The security on the door was to stop people getting in, not out. I looked to the side. There it was, a palm-sized black panel set into the wall. That had to be an override for the door. What I didn't know was whether it would set off an alarm as well as opening the door.

Option one: press it and see.

Option two: get Paula's toolkit out, and apply what little I knew about intrusion.

Given how little that was, option two was as likely to lead to tripping an alarm as option one. And it would take longer.

I pressed the panel with one fist while pushing the door.

It swung open. Silently.

I paused inside the entrance, listening, catching my breath, and adjusting my hudglasses. Ideally I should shut the door after I left so anyone walking past wouldn't realise anything was amiss but with no external handle –

Then I remembered why not having Paula McIntyre any more could scupper the job.

The next part of the plan involved riding an elevator to the building's basement. Paula would have bypassed the lift security, that being, as I'd just reminded myself, outside my area of expertise. Perhaps if I could raise Nico he could hack the lift from his end, but even if he wasn't tied up with his own prep, our comms were deliberately low powered to avoid detection, and there was a lot of Martian rock between me and him. Perhaps if I stood at the top of the lift shaft and he happened to be standing at the bottom… Might as well try shouting.

My mind went blank for a moment. *Think.* There would be a way out of this.

Just like the external doors, any elevators giving access outside the complex needed a pass. Therefore, all I actually had to do was get hold of a staff pass. There: a simple solution, at least in theory. I called up the map on my hud.

The senior staff would all be out enjoying the New Year's celebrations but some of the up-and-coming execs would be happy to work overtime to prove their worth. I needed to head into less exclusive territory.

I kept my eyes and ears open, pausing at every corner, taking a slow, stealthy path through the corridors of corporate power. Even if nothing we'd done so far had tripped any alarms, it was only a matter of time before I ran into more guards, or someone noticed the open door to the Celestial Colonnades.

Despite the need to concentrate on the here and now, Paula McIntyre's parting words haunted me.

In order to know Mr Lau she must work for Everlight. So why would she help steal their greatest prize?

Firstly, because she didn't know I was after the Eye until we were deep inside the Everlight complex.

Once she knew she could have 'accidently' tripped an alarm, or alerted the guards who passed us by. Why hadn't she? But I remembered her response to the Colonnade doors, and to the security on the Eye. She was proud of her work. She wanted to know she could defeat Everlight's security.

Which would be odd if she worked for them. But I suspected Paula McIntyre was what her file claimed: an independent security specialist. And she was working for Mr Lau.

He'd probably sent her here to keep tabs on me. Maybe I should be flattered. She might have had a hand in Xiao Fei's fate – or that might have been coincidence. They did happen.

It was safe to assume she wasn't here officially. No doubt my ex-boss had his own reasons for following me beyond the ends of the Earth. He might even have been after the Eye himself; imagine if Everlight had lost the Eye of Heaven, only to have it returned by prompt action from the agent of a relatively minor exec. How much face would Mr Lau have saved his employers then? When it came to shafting colleagues, the criminal underworld could learn a lot from the corps.

Good job I had no plans to return to the day-job.

Fortunately, the money from this job would buy a new face and a watertight identity, and thanks to Mr P, I already had a means of getting off-planet. Assuming I could trust Mr P. And assuming I could get myself and the Eye of Heaven out of Everlight's territory.

What was that?

I was still in exec country, and didn't expect anyone to be behind the door the odd sound had come from. Given it was labelled with a masculine name – and no job title, which always signified high status, because if you had to ask, you were too lowly to know – the nature of the sound was also a surprise. A girlish giggle. And there it was again: more of a moan this time. Interesting. Whilst I could imagine our self-important exec getting himself some off-the-record female company for the New Year, I'd have expected them to get a room rather than use his office. It wasn't as though Mars didn't have nice hotels ideal for enjoying sex with all the trimmings.

I listened a little longer, and heard more faint sounds of pleasure. Then I pressed the pad. The door opened; I'd half expected there to be security on this door to an important man's office, but if there was it'd been disabled. I paused out of sight, though from the sound of it no one had noticed me. Poking my head round the open door I saw a familiar layout: a small office/antechamber with some hardcopy storage, an uncomfortable waiting area and a desk for the office administrator, then a doorway through to the main, larger, office. The noises came from the main office. I crept up to the open doorway, staying out of line-of-sight, although from the sound of it, whoever was inside was unlikely to notice me. Definitely a young woman enjoying herself. Even so, I drew my gun.

Peering round the door from a low vantage-point, I found myself looking across plush carpet to a desk whose size and pretentious build rivalled Mr Lau's. A young Chinese woman perched on the front of the desk. Her head was thrown back and she was panting in delight, no doubt thanks to the attentions of the young man in a brown uniform kneeling on the ground in front of her, his head buried deep her crotch.

I suspected neither of them was the owner of this office.

Looking around I spotted a couple of anomalous items on the otherwise immaculate plum-coloured carpet. That small dark scrap of fabric had to be underwear but there was also a smart jacket with, if my eyes didn't deceive me, the corner of an ID badge peeking out of a fold.

I had no desire to interrupt the kind of fun I hoped to be

having myself in the none-too-distant future so I kept low and crept forward, heading for the discarded jacket.

I'd almost reached it when the woman's cries ramped up a notch. I looked up to see her hands deep in the boy's hair, her gaze fixed forward and her mouth open in a wide O set to become a squeal of pure animal pleasure at any moment.

At which point she spotted me.

Her gaze sharpened, and she gave a wholly different type of squeal. Her hands pushed away and, tangled as they were in the boys' hair, shoved him backwards. I acted on instinct. My dart hit him in the back and he fell to one side.

The woman stared at me. I waited for her to make another noise but she looked too terrified to even breathe. Which made sense: in my camo'd suit I was a disembodied head with wraparound shades and, if she looked closely, a floating gun.

'I'm not going to hurt you,' I said in Mandarin. With my free hand I pulled my hudglasses up into my forehead. Maintaining a disguise was pointless now, thanks to having left Ms McIntyre alive and able to identify me, and showing this young woman I was an ordinary woman, albeit in a skinsuit, might stop her suffering a heart attack on the spot.

In a tiny, terrified voice she croaked, 'You shot Bao.'

'Yes, with tranq.' I looked over at the unconscious boy sprawled at her feet. Now I could see the uniform I confirmed my initial impression that he worked in Everlight's mailroom. 'He'll be fine.'

'Oh. Right. Of course.' I suspected she would agree with anything I said. She'd probably never been so frightened in her life.

I should shoot her too, then take her pass and be done with it, but I didn't feel good about this. 'Listen, I'm sorry I... sorry I interrupted you. And Bao.'

'That's all right.' She sounded incredulous, like she couldn't imagine the scary creature I appeared to be ever being sorry about anything.

'I need your pass now. That's why I came in.'

'My pass? I... Why?'

'Do you really want to know?'

She looked stricken and shook her head. 'No. You're right. I don't want to know.'

'Listen, can I ask you something?'

She nodded, confused.

'Is this your boss' office?' I recognised that dress sense. She wore clothes I might have chosen myself, right down to the black lace panties under the conservative skirt and blouse.

She nodded again, and bit her lip.

'And is he a smug and smiling bastard who wants you at his beck-and-call twenty-four seven, expects you to deal with his cock-ups and is happy to take credit for your hard work?'

For a moment a different type of shock flitted across her face. Then she grimaced, and nodded.

'Reminds me of someone I know. You know what?' I gestured at the unconscious boy, 'I really wish I'd done something like this in *his* office.'

She smiled, and blushed. Which was rather charming.

'I am going to have to take your pass now.'

'I understand.' As I reached for her jacket she said, 'Wait. If you're trying to leave, it won't be enough.'

'What do you mean?'

'They've upped security for the New Year. Because of the public coming in. You need a scan as well as a pass to get anywhere.'

'Scan as in palm or iris?'

'Depends where you're trying to go. Oh. I shouldn't have told you that, should I?' Was that a smile?

'You didn't. I threatened you with torture when your pass didn't get me out.'

'You... Oh, I see. Where do you need to get to?'

'Garage level.'

'I'll show you. Just let me get my...'she gestured at the

discarded panties.

I let her lead the way. Worst case, she tried to run or set off an alarm, in which case she'd get tranqed and dragged to the door. I didn't really expect that to happen, and it didn't. At the elevator she gave me her pass and pointed to the palm-print reader beside it. 'I suppose you have to shoot me once I've opened the door for you.'

'Afraid so.'

'Will it hurt?'

'You'll hardly feel it.'

The elevator ride down was interminable. I'd opened a comm channel and pinged Nico and Gregori, but only got a reply as the doors opened onto the garage level. Gregori was striding towards the lift, while Nico stood a few paces back, next to a battered tunnelbug.

'I was getting worried,' said Gregori, arms open.

'You got what we came for?' Nico called out a moment later.

'I did.' I evaded Gregori's attempt at a bear-hug.

Gregori frowned at me. 'And what is it we have stolen, exactly?'

I jerked a thumb over my shoulder to indicate my backpack. 'The Eye of Heaven.'

Nico laughed. 'That's fifty you owe me, *dost*!'

'Huh!' Gregori huffed. 'So where is Ms McIntyre?'

'I have some bad news regarding Ms McIntyre. Turns out we were right to be suspicious of her.'

'But the job's not blown?' Nico's smiled faltered.

A siren began to wail.

'Oh,' said Gregori, grinning, 'it is it New Year already?'

'No Gregori,' I shouted above the alarm, 'it is trouble already.'

'What, I cannot make joke to defuse the tension?'

'Yes, you can, but let's get a move on, huh?'

Nico had the three near-identical tunnelbugs parked next to each other, hotwired and good to go. As Gregori turned to get in the middle of the three I grabbed his arm and pointed to his head. 'Hood.'

'What?'

'Pull your skinsuit hood up. No time for wardrobe adjustments at the other end.'

'Da. Of course.' He did so.

'But save the rebreather.'

'I do know how to survive on Mars!'

He looked cute when peeved. I leaned across to give him a peck on the cheek. 'Impress me, stud-muffin,' I whispered. Then, over the comm to both of them, 'See you on the other side!'

Nico raised a hand before climbing into his vehicle.

I pulled myself up into my tunnelbug, threw myself into the seat, slapped the panel to shut the door, and grabbed the wheel.

It wasn't exactly a racing start.

First off, we had to queue to leave the garage – currently dark, unmonitored and with an open door, thanks to Nico's earlier efforts. Nico first, then me, then Gregori.

As soon as we were in the main tunnel outside, we split up. Nico and I went left, nominally the 'out' direction, though I peeled off into a smaller service tunnel after a hundred metres. Gregori broke right, heading back towards Olympus City.

One of the oldest scams in the book is the shell game. Some guy in a cave probably came up with it: three shells and a pea, guess which shell the pea's under. In that form, the point is to fool the mark using sleight of hand. In this version, the Eye was with me for the duration, and the solid rock of the tunnels meant we couldn't even communicate between vehicles, let alone swap cargo, but having three targets still meant a two-in-three chance any pursuers would pick the wrong one. We were upping the odds of getting the loot, and at least one of us, out.

I'd have preferred the odds with zero pursuers, but from the sound of that parting alarm, our luck had run out. Whether it had been the open door to the Colonnades, the unconscious secretary or someone coming across one of Nico's hacks, we were blown.

I felt oddly calm. Must have been adrenalin comedown. Plus, I'd driven this route half a dozen times during our practice runs, although I wasn't going to assume I knew which turns to take. I kept an eye on the inertial nav readout in the corner of my hud.

Thanks to the load on my back, I had to hunch forward in the seat, but I wasn't going to be parted from the prize. From now on everything had to go like clockwork.

The view through the tunnelbug's front screen showed rock: rock below, rock to each side, rock above. The others would have a similar view, though Nico and Gregori were sticking to larger tunnels, because they were the diversion, roles they weren't delighted with. But they were the best drivers, and I was the one with the Eye. They'd draw attention while I sneaked out under the radar. Nico's path would take him straight towards the surface, before jinking off along a lateral tunnel; anyone trying to predict his course should be thrown by this change of direction. Should be. Gregori was doing the really fancy driving, heading directly towards the domes as though about to burst into Olympus Central itself, then doubling back. Which left me to creep upwards through the oldest, narrowest tunnels.

I slowed as my nav readout showed a bottleneck ahead; now the rock above was barely higher than the 'bug's roof, and its treads weren't getting much purchase on the tunnel's narrow bore. But I knew I'd make it, because we'd practiced this, several times.

I was just ramping up the speed again – insofar as tunnelbugs have speed to ramp up – when the vehicle's comm crackled. I didn't think I was near enough to any inhabited area to get random signal bleed through the rock, but I could hope.

'…unauthorised … please identify ….'

Some hope.

I resisted the urge to speed up. I knew how fast it was safe to take these tunnels, and that's how fast I was going. And I was over halfway now.

At the next fork, I went left. Fifty-fifty chance they'd go right, I told myself. But this was a long straight tunnel, and before the next turn, lights bobbed into view behind me. The transmission came clear. 'Kindly stop your vehicle, and prepare to present your credentials.' I turned the radio off. It wasn't going to tell me anything I didn't already know.

Only two turns to go now. As the tunnel arced round, I ramped the tunnelbug's speed up. This tunnel had the steepest slope so far, and between that and the excessive speed, the 'bug began to yaw, until I wasn't on the tunnel bottom any more, but creeping up the leftmost wall. Scary, but it seemed stable enough. Except the next turn was to the right. I eased off, and for a moment the 'bug lost grip, and slid. I grabbed the dashboard, braced to spin or flip, but the very narrowness of the tunnel saved me. The 'bug fishtailed, then stabilised. I took the right turn.

Another turn, in only fifty metres, and then I was on the home straight to, if not safety, then at least a way to lose the current pursuer. I took the turn. Lights flashed round the corner only a few seconds behind me. Much as my instinct was to floor the 'bug, I needed to slow down, even as those headlights grew in my monitor. Easing off had my nerves screaming but, I reminded myself, they'd have to slow down too. We were about to hit the end of the line. I tried not to think about how exposed I'd be when that happened. In tunnels this old, and this far from the city, we were out of the realms of automation; making my escape required some good old manual intervention.

Up ahead, the tunnel ended in a metal box.

I drove into the airlock too fast, and slammed on the brakes. My 'bug bumped the outer door, throwing me half out my seat, then stalled. I switched my hud to lo-light as I jumped out. The oncoming headlights became a blinding sun. Looked as if I'd be doing this by touch, not sight. I dialled my vision back down. I knew what I was looking for; I'd done this before, I'd be fine.

My first slap hit blank metal. I coughed; the air was full of the rock-dust I'd kicked up. The oncoming lights were about to run me over. On my second attempt, I hit the button. The inner door slammed down a handbreadth from my face.

The airlock was windowless. I was in near darkness, the only light coming from the tunnelbug's cab. I dialled my vision up and stumbled round the 'bug. The air was frigid but I felt a glow on my exposed cheek as I passed the wheeled tracks. I'd run this tunnelbug hard.

Over at the outer door, I hit the command to start the lock cycling. Then I remembered what I'd forgotten in the panic of the oncoming lights. I pulled myself up onto the treads and leaned in through the door to grab a flat cylinder the size of my palm from the 'bug's dash. And paused. After the incident at the practice airlock Nico had reduced the amount in his charges to what he called 'just enough bang to do the job'. Which meant the charge had to be stuck in *exactly* the right place: centre bottom of the outer airlock door, ready to activate as the airlock opened and do enough damage to disable the airlock without trashing the tunnelbug or broaching the inner door. Good plan, except that the middle bottom of this airlock door was, thanks to my irresponsible parking, no longer accessible. I had to back the 'bug up. Heart beating in my ears I threw myself into the driver's seat and hit the start button.

Nothing happened.

Of course: Nico'd had to hotwire the tunnelbugs to get them working.

In the grim silence, something clanged behind me. My pursuers were knocking on the back door. Great.

And my head hurt. Why did my head hurt...?

I looked up through the 'bug's screen to see the status readout on the airlock control panel click down to three out of five bars. And the 'bug door was still open.

I pulled on the lose flap of skinsuit under my chin, rolling the fabric up to cover my nose and mouth. This made a seal with my hudglasses, activating the suit's rebreather function. Some of the fog cleared from my brain.

Nico had hotwired the tunnelbugs because he didn't have valid Everlight ID. But I did. The downtrodden administrator's pass was still around my neck. I fumbled it onto the ID scanner and pressed 'start'.

A gentle hum filled the cab. I slammed the 'bug into reverse, doing an abrupt start-stop, then grabbed the limpet-charge and half-fell out the 'bug door.

The airlock readout hit one bar.

I bent down and slapped the charge onto the lower lip of the airlock, then leapt back into the tunnelbug. As I hit the control to close the cab door the airlock slid up, flooding my vision with watery sunlight.

The charge went off.

The world vibrated and small bits of debris began to rain down. A feeble puff of dust fanned in through the cab door before it sealed.

I gunned the throttle. The tunnelbug lurched forward through a fall of dust and small rocks, bursting out into the Martian dawn.

I made myself breathe slowly and set my hud display to daylight acuity, with overlaid map. During my recent acrobatics my pack, with its heavy, precious cargo, had acted as an impromptu and brutal massage stone. I'd have some great bruises.

I turned the tunnelbug slowly; though rated for the Martian (lack of) atmosphere, 'bugs are designed for use on the flat and there was little of that to be had now I was out on Olympus itself. After getting this far it would be embarrassing to flip my vehicle.

I spared a look at Nico's handiwork as I drove back past the airlock. A gaping hole with dust still billowing out of it. Result. No one would be following me out that way.

Our routes through the tunnels all wended upwards, but now I needed to head directly upslope. If we did have anyone on our tails out here, they'd be coming from the lower levels, which gave us a head start. Plus, they wouldn't expect us to head up, towards the distant crater rim. After all, there was no escape route that way, was there?

Well, there'd better be. I took the chance to look around, and up. Another lovely clear Martian day. Bright now; brighter later. Hopefully. And somewhere up there was the Rainfall comet, in its corporate shroud.

No one else down here, which was a relief. I had no way of knowing whether the pursuit vehicle currently stuck behind the broken airlock happened to be in the right place at the right time, was just quick off the mark when we tripped the alarm or was in possession of advance info. I didn't know whether Nico and Gregori had been pursued either.

I'd set my suit set to ping the others. Nothing yet. Not that I expected to hear from them for a while, given how far apart our various exit points had been.

I turned the 'bug radio back on. Nothing but static. I breathed a little easier.

My suit pinged me. No voice, just a ping, but I knew what it meant. I smiled and looked up the slope. The ground was steeper here, as my 'bug crawled farther up the great expanse of Olympus' skirts, but we'd chosen this route because it was relatively free of crevasses, broken ground or other obstacles. I couldn't see anything that wasn't red and rocky on the slope ahead, and there was no anomalous outline on the horizon. But I hadn't really expected to see much.

I was nearly on the flyer before I got a visual. Its identifying pings had been getting more frequent, and its looming bulk had also appeared on my hud, if not in the real world.

Two days ago Mr P, or more likely another of his agents, had flown into Olympus airspace on, I'm sure, legitimate business. Or more likely, pleasure, taking advantage of Mount Olympus' legendary thermals. They'd swooped in using two large, slow gliders, no threat to anyone, and stayed clear of any areas which might be considered sensitive by the authorities. The fact that only one glider had left after this harmless leisure jaunt had gone unremarked; Mr P had confirmed that no one had taken an interest before we set off. Obviously he couldn't be sure the flyer hadn't been found since, but given it was powered down, under a mimetic cloth making it invisible unless you were practically standing on it and its transponder had only awoken in response to my suit's ping, I had high hopes. Hopes now realised.

Still nothing from the others. I drove the 'bug up to the camo sheet, snuggling in close on the upslope side. If no one else made the rendezvous I'd have to fly out by myself. Shiv had given me a few flying lessons back on Earth and I'd topped up with a single sim-session here but if it came to it, I'd be relying on the autopilot. I could hear Shiv's voice now, telling me how anyone could pilot a flyer, if they were willing to trust their lives to a machine and not try anything fancy. Unfortunately, the next part of the plan required something fancy. Shiv had gone on to say, laughing, how flying was like driving except as well as stop/go and left/right you also had to allow for up/down. He'd said it took skill to master that, implying he had that skill. But he'd died in a vehicle like this.

No room for that kind of thinking. I could mope later, when I was safe.

The mimetic fabric covering the flyer was an LM invention, though I'm not sure whether they also came up with the dissolution catalyst; always preferred making than breaking, those Deimon founders.

A yellow warning appeared in the corner of my hud. Five minutes oxygen remaining. Of course: the original plan was to keep the 'bugs pressurised; my rebreather saved me after the cock-up in the airlock but it was designed for emergency use only, in this case getting from bug to flyer. It was about to fail. Good job there was another source of breathable air around here.

But I had to hurry.

The dis-cat for the mimetic fabric was a short rod; along with the limpet-charges, we'd each been issued with one, and I grabbed mine from the tunnelbug's tool pouch. I took the rod, wrapped a corner of the fabric round it and held it in place, waiting for the reaction to start. Seconds later the rod glowed and vibrated. I let go and stepped back.

It worked fast. One moment I was standing next to a massive, odd shaped rock, then, with a speed my eyes worked hard to follow, the fabric covering just disappeared, unravelling to constituent molecules and blowing away in the wind, to reveal a four-person flyer.

As I stepped back to admire our penultimate form of transport my suit pinged. Gregori. About time.

'Everything all right?' I asked over the suit's com.

'I attracted some attention.'

'But you lost them, yes?' I moved round the flyer, looking for the hatch.

'Oh yes. I had great fun.'

Of course he did. Did this boy take anything seriously? 'You've not had any trouble since you left the tunnels?' *Here we are.* The hatch opened directly onto the tiny cockpit with its four skeletal mesh-seats. An actual airlock would have been too much additional weight in a vehicle like this.

'Some chatter on the radio, but no one knows where we are.'

I begged to differ. Orbital eyes would have been scanning for us as soon as we broke cover – some friendly, some not. And the unfriendly ones wouldn't take long to spot the uncovered flyer. 'Fine. We need to get going.'

'Nico is not here?' Gregori said as he swung his tunnelbug around to park next to mine.

'Not yet.'

'Should we leave him?'

I was tempted. We were on a clock. Hell, *I* was on a clock: I could only pressurize the flyer cabin when we were all inside. But

we wouldn't have got this far without our smiling ex-soldier.
'Only if we…' my suit pinged. 'Nico, that you?'

'Yeah. Sorry. Had to take a diversion.'

'You were followed?' Not him too.

'No, it was a tunnel closure, some issue with those crappy old tunnels, y'know?'

'Right. Let's get a move on!'

I took the seat next to Gregori; Nico climbed aboard a few dozen seconds later and sat behind. Even with one person missing, the cockpit felt crowded. As soon as Gregori shut the door I hit the O2 release. As the cabin began to pressurize my rebreather status hit red. I held my breath. I knew the timings: the cabin would only take thirty seconds to full atmosphere. A very long thirty seconds. Twin tides of darkness began to edge in from the corners of my vision.

The cabin pressure light lit green.

I yanked the rebreather off and took a massive, gasping breath. Gregori, who'd been prepping for take-off, rolled his own suit down and took a more measured one, then grinned at me. 'We are ready to go. I advise everyone to strap in!'

Before I could take Gregori's advice I had to get my backpack off. In the cramped conditions I ended up with it on my lap, hugging the Eye to my chest.

The flyer vibrated as the engines kicked in. Only minimal power was required to launch in this gravity, just a couple of old-fashioned but sturdy props tucked under each wing. And we faced downslope, giving us a head start.

We shot off the side of Olympus Mons like the proverbial excrement off a spade.

Nico whistled, whether in surprise or appreciation I wasn't sure.

Once my guts had caught up with the rest of my body I said, 'No fancy stunts, Gregori. Just get us to the rendezvous as fast as you can.'

'Aye-aye!' He banked the craft in a long loop; we needed to

come round to follow the slope of the mountain, up, up and away.

The radio hissed, then a bored female voice said, 'Calling unidentified craft on the southeast quadrant, bearing two-six-one. This is Olympus Central ATC. Do you read us?'

Of course traffic control would be wanting a word. I was more concerned about parties who wouldn't announce themselves.

I shook my head to confirm we wouldn't be answering that hail. 'Anyone else out here?' I asked Gregori.

'Two other flyers.'

'What sort of flyers? How far away?' Actually only one thing mattered. 'Have they got the height on us?'

'Wait... One is higher up the slope than us, but farther round, to the west. They have recently launched I think. The other is well below us, heading away.'

'And are they powered?'

'I am not sure. The closest one, it is a small craft, so it must be, da.'

This was actually good news. On Earth, air superiority is about thrust and manoeuvrability. On Mars, with its thin air and low gravity, what matters is sustainable lift. As with the tunnelbugs, we'd had to work with standard off-the-shelf civilian tech. But size was on our side. This flyer was big but light. It had a lot of surface area – a lot of lift. And we'd be getting some extra help.

I turned to Gregori. 'Can we lose the engines yet?'

'Not yet. A little more height....'

'And what's that nearby flyer doing now?'

'Ah. I think it is trying to intercept us.'

'And will it succeed?'

'Not if I can help it.'

I left it at that. It wasn't as though we were built for complex evasive manoeuvres, but I'd hired Gregori for his piloting skills. If anyone could lose them, he could. We banked hard right, spiralling upwards.

The traffic controller repeated her request, less bored and more annoyed. I told Gregori to block the transmission.

Below us, the vast slopes of Olympus Mons scrolled past. It was possible to imagine we were flying on the flat, towards a distant horizon, rather than up the side of a geological feature big enough to swallow a small country.

Above us, unseen and – hopefully – undetected, something interesting was happening. Well, a couple of things, one routine and the other highly unusual.

'We are high enough that the engines are of little use now, Ms C.' I insisted Gregori called me that, despite what we got up to outside work hours.

'Then let's ditch them.' And hope our friends in orbit are ready – both of them.

'What is that English saying? Chocks away!'

The flyer shuddered, dipped, then bucked upwards. Gregori had detached the four prop engines, leaving them to tumble down to the red slope below us. In doing so he'd jettisoned half the flyer's net weight, excluding passengers. Back on the surface this vehicle would now be light enough that, had it not had a footprint the size of a circus big top, the three of us might have lifted it between us. By reducing our weight this way we'd just added five percent to our lift and speed. Possibly more, given Mr P had come up with that figure based on there being four of us in the flyer; perhaps Ms McIntyre's betrayal had a small upside. But we needed an additional advantage to ensure a clean getaway.

And that, finally, was where our tech teen in space came in.

The grand plan, when humans first settled Mars, had been to terraform it. One of the first acts of the proto-government of Mars – a council of corporate interests plus some national representatives – had been to establish the Mars Terraforming Treaty, which sounded grand and effective but hadn't amounted to much so far. Terraforming was a vague and over-ambitious plan which no one country or corp would take the lead on – as witnessed by schemes like Project Rainfall, where what could have been a game-changer in making Mars habitable had become a source of short-term profit for one company. But some projects had been completed over the years under the auspices of the MTT: atmospheric enrichment schemes, introduction of tailored organisms like the hardy-lichens, and, most ambitious of all, the orbital mirrors. How much the space-mirrors at both poles and in geostationary orbit over the Tharsis region actually warmed the planet was still debated, and the payments that corps and nations grudgingly made to maintain the MTT barely covered their upkeep, but they were up there. And they were, apparently, hackable.

Ana should have taken control of the Tharsis mirror overnight, and had it refocused ready for dawn. But we were dealing with slow physical processes here, undetectable save by their knock-on effects. If I knew how bright a Martian morning usually was I could maybe have seen, or used my hudglasses to see, what Ana's efforts were achieving, but I didn't. I had to take her part in the plan on trust.

'How's that pursuing craft looking, Gregori?'

'I think we are losing them.'

'You *think* we're losing them?'

'They are keeping pace with us, so they must have highly efficient engines. Ah, wait.'

'Don't tell me: they've transformed into a glider too?'

'No. But we are being contacted.'

'By our pursuer?'

'The caller is not using a transponder but yes, the signal originates from that direction.'

'Oh go on then. Might as well hear what they've got to say.' It would take my mind off worrying about whether Ana was doing her job. We were in her hands now, hers and Gregori's.

'I assume I am speaking to Ms Choi?' A male voice, speaking perfect Mandarin.

I was past lying. But I was also past negotiating. 'Assume

what you like. How can we help you?'

'It is more how we can help you.'

'We're doing fine actually.'

'I am not sure the same can be said of your mother.'

'My… What are you talking about?'

'Ms Choi, I know it is a long way to Luna, and our influence there is not as great as on Mars, but I am sure you –'

'Wait up. You – on behalf of Everlight I assume – are about to tell me that if I turn myself in you'll, what, arrange for her to go free?'

'Actually it was more stick than carrot, as the saying goes. If you do not give up the Eye now, then we have contacts on Luna who may –'

'No.'

'Do you understand what I am suggesting?'

'You're not suggesting, you're threatening. Or possibly blackmailing. And I'm not having any of it.' I reached across and cut the transmission.

I didn't feel good about my decision, but it was possible harm for my mother versus ending up in prison myself, along with my accomplices; assuming Everlight even bothered with due process. If they did hurt Mum, I'd have a load of guilt to deal with, but deal I would. I wouldn't blow the job, and betray my compatriots, on the chance Everlight would make good on their implied threat.

Gregori was looking at me like it was his mother I'd just condemned. 'What?' I snapped.

'I only wished to tell you, we are now higher and faster than I have ever been!'

No, it wasn't angst or condemnation, just that charming boyish excitement, bless him. And he wasn't wrong. Several readouts were near their max. More strikingly, the view ahead showed a dark sky beyond the false horizon of the mountain; although were still on Olympus' slopes, we were approaching the edge of Mars' atmosphere. 'That's fantastic. And have we lost the pursuit?'

'They are falling back. No one can catch us now, not with this speed and altitude.'

Had our pursuers launched a glider, that being what this flyer was now, then they too might have taken advantage of the exceptional thermal lift we were now getting off the expansive slopes of the solar system's largest mountain, as heated up by the solar system's largest space mirror. But they'd sent a small powered craft after us. And now the atmosphere was too thin for its engines, and we'd left it for dead. Despite the hiccups, the plan had worked. The final rendezvous was imminent.

'I am sorry about this.'

It took me a moment to register who'd spoken. I turned in my seat to see Nico pointing a large gun at me. 'Oh for... Seriously? Am I going to meet anyone today who *doesn't* work for Everlight?'

'I don't!' chirped Gregori, oblivious of this latest double-cross.

'And nor do I.'

'Really, Nico? Then what is going on?'

Beside me, Gregori turned in his seat and saw what Nico was holding. 'Oh,' he murmured, then turned back and hunched down, like making himself small enough might save him.

'Please do as I say now, Ms C. I will tell you where to land this craft.'

He was nervous, which was both understandable and potentially useful. 'I think you owe us an explanation first. You're not Everlight so who... is it the Triads?'

'They have my wife and child. I must do as they say.'

My mind started working out ways we could solve this, some course of action that allowed us to save Nico's family without blowing the job. Then I caught myself. 'You're divorced; your ex-wife is on Earth. And you have no children.'

He smiled his winning smile. 'You have me there. I thought you would do your research, but it was worth a try. Families can be our weak points, can't they?'

'And to think I liked you, Nico.'

'You know it is nothing personal.'

'Like murdering my brother was nothing personal?'

'I did not murder your brother.'

'But the Triads did.' He didn't deny it so I carried on, both to buy us time and because I had to know. 'Why did they kill him?'

'We only wanted to talk to him. He refused to co-operate, and tried to break free. His flyer was too badly damaged to land.'

That 'we'. I'd been carrying Earther assumptions about the Triads not letting gwailo be more than runners, but Nico must be in deep with them; deep enough that his connections hadn't shown up in my, or Ika's, searches. Cross 'offer him double' off my short list of options. 'Why did you want to talk to him?'

'Our patron is very secretive. And you have been very discreet. This is why I had to wait until now to act.'

'Thanks for getting our hopes up, Nico. And now we've done your dirty work you'll take the Eye of Heaven and blame us for the theft?'

'Very good again!'

'I thought you and Everlight were on the same side. Approximately.'

'They will be glad to get this object back, from whatever source. You don't even know what you've really done today. Enough talking I think. Gregori, stop trying to fly us higher, and bring us down at the location I will provide.'

Gregori, who had been making subtle moves over the flyer's console, raised his hands.

'Or what?' I demanded. 'You'll shoot us?'

'I can fly this vehicle myself if I have to, Ms Choi.'

'I was thinking more about the risk of damaging it. That's a heavy needler, isn't it? You do know how thin the membrane on this flyer is?'

'A stungun would be no good against your skinsuit. As for damaging the flyer,' he lunged forward, and pressed the needler against Gregori's ear, 'it depends where the shot goes first.'

I have, since that day, worked through what happened next many times.

Firstly, I shouted, 'No!' How much of that was down to general stress and how much down to the threat against the man I was sleeping with I don't know. Bit of both, I suspect.

Gregori threw himself forward. Again, I don't know if that was a response to my shout or to Nico's action or, most probably, a bit of both.

At moments like this everything becomes both so slow that every second is loaded with possibilities and so inevitable that you can't do more than acknowledge those possibilities as they unfold. Nothing you do at the time, or later, will make any difference.

I'd love to report that my cute and dippy lover was, in fact, a master martial artist, and that he'd only been playing along with Nico, ready to react once he had the traitor's undivided attention, slipping out of the line of fire to come up, somehow, in the impossibly small space between the three of us, then disabling Nico with a single killing strike. But he wasn't. And he was still wearing his safety harness. He must have forgotten that. As a result he only ducked forward a little way before the harness caught him.

It wasn't far enough. When Nico fired most of the supersonic needles hit their mark, and turned the back of Gregori's head to bloody pulp.

At this point I took physical action, without any intervention from my conscious mind.

Nico's head was between my and Gregori's seat. I hefted the Eye of Heaven off my lap and rammed it back over my shoulder like a reverse shot-put, into Nico's face. I heard his skull crack. The Eye, in its pack, slipped out of my hand, but Nico had fallen backwards, and wasn't making any noise.

There was a noise in here though. A sharp hiss.

Beyond where Gregori dangled in his harness the side window showed an unpleasant spatter pattern of red and grey —

and black. A peppering of holes covered an area the span of two hands. The window hadn't shattered, but it was holed. And we all know what that means.

If I could have spared the breath I might have sworn then.

I stared at the flight console. I had enough basic knowledge to... to what? I wasn't sure. I grabbed the joystick. It didn't move. When I put a hand on the throttle panel it stayed dark. I touched, then hit, a couple more controls. Nothing. I was locked out.

Poor Gregori hadn't been a martial artist but he'd known his way around vehicles. His response to Nico trying to take over this one had been to lock the controls. Smart move. No, stupid move.

The darkness at the edges of my vision began to creep back.

A small green light started blinking near to top left of the console. I wondered what that meant. It didn't mean the atmosphere was fine, because it wasn't.

I had to do something. I had no idea what. I wasn't sure my body would obey me anyway.

At least, I thought, this makes sense now. I know how and why Shiv died. And I'd learnt a lesson on how the Triads operate here, though there was something Nico said, about not knowing what we'd really done, something I still didn't get. I hate loose ends.

The darkness met in the middle and I was yanked up to heaven.

Six

Waking up was a surprise.

It was gradual, and I spent a while getting a feel for my body – which ached, but worked – before I risked opening my eyes. From the gravity it felt as if I was on Mars. Given recent events, being on Mars wasn't a good thing. Beat being dead, though.

I screwed up my face, then opened my eyes. Everything felt muzzy and slow, like I'd slept too long.

I lay on a bed in the middle of a grassy plain; to my left the sun was setting in orange and gold. It had to be a projection, but it was a good one. I could even feel a grass-scented breeze.

A slender man in loose green clothing sat on a seat next to my bed. When I focused on him, he smiled down at me.

'Hello there. I expect you have questions.'

He wasn't wrong. 'Who are you?'

'I'm Sam Matheson, although we're not very formal here, so just Sam will do. You like to be called Lizzie, yes?'

'Yes.' His last name registered. 'Am I on Deimos?'

'You sure are.'

He had a sort-of American accent. Which made sense, given the original Deimos Collective were Americans who left a couple of decades before that country ceased to exist. 'Right.' I could see past the evening scene projected around me now; I was in a small, square room. 'And are you Mr P?'

'The man behind the job? Yep. That's me. And I was very impressed with how you carried it out, given the various setbacks.'

'Yeah, about that. Why aren't I dead?'

'You were, for a while. Your heart had stopped by the time we picked you up, and you were seconds away from brain-death.'

'I... Just how *did* you pick me up?'

'The skyhook worked fine, even though your end of it was automated.'

'Right,' I said again, trying to think past the cotton wool in my brain. The plan had been for an orbital lifter to dip to its lowest operational altitude just as our flyer reached its highest operation altitude. The lifter would snatch our flyer from the top of Mars' atmosphere. A bit like those fishing eagles on old documentaries snatching a fish out the water, although that didn't end too well for the fish. Also, in this case, at the last moment the flyer would release a balloon, giving it that last bit of lift, and providing a tether for the lifter to snag. The lifter had a flexible docking rig to get us out of our flimsy vehicle, at which point I'd have handed over the Eye, and the lifter would have taken us to the orbital station or moon of our choice.

Unless I was in a particularly cruel and unimaginative afterlife, the lifter had picked up the flyer, so someone must've made contact then set a course to the orbital rendezvous. My final sensation of being hurled heavenwards had been the jolt as the balloon released.

'Gregori.'

'I'm sorry?'

'Our pilot, his name was Gregori.' I had to ask, even though I knew. 'Did he... He didn't make it, did he?'

'I'm afraid not. When we made contact with the flyer he opened a one-way channel while he prepped for the pickup. We heard what happened.'

'So what about...?'

'Your other companion survived.'

Shame. 'And where is he now?' If Nico was anywhere I could get to him, he'd better be well enough to run.

'We ejected him.'

I stared at Mr P – Sam. 'Really? Thought you Deimons were pacifists.'

Sam laughed, a little bashful. He was about Gregori's age, and more informal in the flesh than his Mr P persona. 'No, not like that. Sorry, I wasn't clear. We patched him up and sent him on his way in a lifepod.'

'Some might say that was a waste of a lifepod.' But Nico had only been doing what he had to do. And getting angry at him wouldn't bring Gregori back.

'Perhaps. We told Everlight where to find him.'

'That's quite… expedient, in its own way.'

'I guess it is.' Sam put his hands on his knees, ready to move. 'If you're up to it, there's something you'll want to see.' 'What sort of something?' Not that I didn't trust him.

'Simpler if I show you. It's not far. Feel free to ask questions on the way.'

I didn't have much choice. I sat up slowly; head a bit fuzzy, but otherwise in good shape.

I declined Sam's offer to help me stand, and got off the bed by myself. He was a good thirty centimetres taller than me. I was dressed in loose trousers and a tunic, both mauve; they felt like natural fabrics. When Sam, who wore the male equivalent in green, saw me checking out my duds he said, 'You're welcome to have the skinsuit back, but it's not in the best condition. Or we can find you something else.'

'This is fine for now.' What wasn't fine were the straps on the side of the bed. They were coiled up into recesses, but I wondered what they were for. 'This is our recovery room,' Sam offered.

'Recovery from what?'

'Simple medical procedures. We've also got open wards and an ICU. We have to be self-sufficient up here, for everything.'

'How many of you live on... I mean *in* Deimos?'

'Five thousand four hundred and sixteen. Follow me, and watch your step. Things are... somewhat in flux right now.'

The door slid open as we approached, giving onto a circular tunnel-cum-corridor with a dark grey walkway down the centre; the walls were coated with a opalescent material which reminded me of the Eye; they glowed, illuminating the corridor. Sam walked alongside me, leaving just enough room to pass a man about my age with Hispanic heritage, who was coming the other way. He wore black and orange – I was reassured to see he wasn't dressed identically to Sam – and carried a small bunch of pale yellow flowers. 'Hi,' he said as he approached.

Sam returned the greeting then added, 'Give your cousin my congratulations, okay?'

'Will do.' And he was gone, having spared me a nod and a smile.

'I lied earlier,' said Sam.

'You did?'

'Yes, the population, as of this morning, is now five thousand four hundred and eighteen. Jaime's cousin had twins.'

The corridor led into a low-G gym, like the one on the ship that had brought me to Mars. The fixed cycles, rowing machines, pull-straps and treadmills were crowded in, and the walls and ceiling were studded with bolts, ratchets, gaps and other obscure fittings.

As we picked our way through the gym equipment a pair of willowy teenage girls walking side-by-side on treadmills smiled and waved; an older man busy bench-pressing what looked like his own bodyweight was too distracted to notice us at first, then called out 'Hiya!'

Everyone seemed very friendly; disconcertingly so, perhaps. Part of me wondered what the catch was. Happy drugs in the aircon? Then again, with the exception of five childhood years at the LunaFree, everywhere I'd lived had either been corporate or, to some degree, criminal. Cynicism came naturally.

Beyond the gym, more white corridors, though after a few metres Sam indicated we needed to head up, climbing a vertical access tube narrower than the corridor; here, the walkway material formed sturdy rungs. I decided to hold fire on more questions until we stopped. I wanted to get a feel for this place. There was something odd here and I couldn't quite work out what in my current state.

At the top of the short tube, we set off again. As we passed a side corridor I caught a whiff of frying chilli and garlic. I stopped and inhaled.

'Oh,' said Sam. 'I guess you must be hungry.'

'Yes, I am.' I had a thought. 'How long have I been unconscious?'

'Three days.'

'You're kidding!'

'Nope. The medics didn't want to wake you until they were sure you'd fully recovered. We'll get you some food soon, I promise.'

We came to a section of corridor where the walkway had been laid over a circular hole.

'You'll need to watch your step here. I'll go first.'

As I followed Sam over I looked down into a shaft similar to the one we'd just climbed up; it was unlit, but it appeared to go off at a diagonal angle. 'What's going on down there?'

'Not a lot. We're remodelling, due to… Well, you'll see. The grandmarms always planned this, but we kind of let the community grow organically. Some corridors are becoming redundant.'

'Redundant because…?' I'd come up with an explanation but it was pretty far-fetched.

'Like I said, you'll see. It really is easier to show you.'

I planned to hold him to that. 'The grandmarms? Are you Lena Matheson's great-grandson?'

'Great grandnephew. Not that being a direct descendant makes me any more or less important than anyone else in the community. Everyone calls them the grandmarms.'

We stopped at a door with the number zero on it, gold on white. The door opened for us, leading into a wide oval room whose walls consisted of wrap-around screens. I was aware of people, and furniture, scattered around, but the view projected across the curved wall in front of me demanded my attention. The Rainfall comet filled half the room, its surface black and glossy in the sunlight; behind it I glimpsed the red curve of Mars.

'O-kay,' I said slowly. 'I'm guessing this is what you wanted to show me, but I could use some context.'

'At the risk of sounding pretentious, you're looking at a real-time feed of history in the making. Can you see the landers?'

'Those bright points?' What looked like two drops of mercury were visible on the comet's dark surface, one near the top, the other at the bottom.

Before Sam could reply a voice called out, 'Imp One payload away.'

I looked over to the speaker, a woman who sat at the oval table in the centre of the room, manipulating a 3-D display. A man sat opposite her, also working hard on what looked like projected trajectories flanked by columns of figures. In the middle of the table sat the Eye of Heaven.

I pointed. 'What's *that* doing here?'

'I'll explain in a minute,' whispered Sam. 'You need to watch now.'

The top bright point was spreading. Recalling my recent experience with the camouflaged flyer I asked, 'You're dissolving the nanowrap?'

The woman spoke again. 'Imp Two dis-cat also away.' That answered my question. The Deimons were about to unwrap Everlight's shrink-wrapped dirty snowball.

A second pale patch appeared at the bottom, spreading over the comet's pitted surface. My brain was chugging away, trying to work out the how and the why, even as I watched the comet being revealed before my eyes. I also registered the noise in here:

a murmur of terse commands and information exchange between the dozen or so people working on consoles and displays around the room; and something else, an odd rhythmic beep phasing in and out of the susurrus of voices.

It only took a couple of minutes for the two pale patches to meet. A minute more and what had been a black spiky shape was a grey-white spiky shape.

The man at the table spoke again, 'Switching Imp functions; prepping for burn.'

I turned to Sam, who was grinning like a loon. 'Now you've unwrapped Everlight's prize comet, what exactly do you plan to do with it?'

'Drive it into the atmosphere. The landers become pushers. Some of it will sublime, hopefully enough to up the atmospheric water content a little bit.'

'And the rest?'

'The bulk of the comet will land in the Helles Basin.'

The MTT had a clause stating that, at some unspecified future point, the participating interests would crash-land enough water onto Mars to form a liquid sea. Helles, lowest point on the planet just as Olympus was the highest, was the obvious place for this, which was why no one was allowed to live there.

'And you're sure it'll make landfall in Helles?'

'We've planned this with a lot of care.'

He'd claimed that about stealing the Eye of Heaven. But that had relied on people who were not what they seemed. I was pretty sure the Deimons were exactly what they seemed. This place reminded me of the LunaFree Community, though cleaner and less crowded. 'It's still going to be... disruptive.'

'We've run a lot of simulations. It'll be coming in slow, and this isn't Earth, with high grav and a dense atmosphere; there's no risk of the old dinosaur-killer scenario. Worst case, we trigger some sandstorms. But rather than have people panic, we've told everyone what we're doing.'

'I bet Everlight were pleased.'

'There's nothing they can do about it now.'

'So the plan was always to let Everlight bring in a comet which you'd then steal?' And there was me thinking I'd pulled off an impressive heist with the Eye.

'We're not stealing it, we're… redistributing it.'

'Very altruistic. I'm surprised Everlight didn't put in countermeasures.'

'They had no idea we could do it.'

'I don't think anyone did. This is a game-changer.'

'We hope so. But that's not what I meant. I mean, they didn't think we had the technology.'

The penny dropped. 'You – I mean your founders – came up with the original nanowrap formula didn't you?'

'Uh-huh.' He was still smiling.

'But not the dis-cat to dissolve it.'

'Right again. Everlight kept tight control of that tech. If we'd tried bringing the comet down while it was wrapped then we could've been looking at the disaster movie scenario after all. We needed to free the water. Allow Rainfall to, well, rain down.'

'And how did you get hold of the dis-cat formula for the nanowrap?'

'You stole it for us.'

I looked over at the speaker, and saw that the woman at the table had pushed her display to one side. She was Caucasian and about my mother's age. Her open expression and plain features, combined with her oatmeal-coloured shift, reminded me of some peasant worker used to toiling in a field, though as a low-grav native she didn't have the build for that. I wasn't fooled about what was on the inside either: hard determination shone in those soft brown eyes. 'Why don't you come and sit down?' She gestured to the free seats around the table.

'All right.' The Deimons had done nothing to deserve my suspicion. Unless you counted upsetting the geopolitical balance of the solar system, but that wasn't personal. 'Thanks.'

As I approached I glanced behind me: the rear half of the

room-screen showed a star field. A floating golden zero marked the exit.

'I'm Marcia. Pleased to meet you, Lizzie.' She gestured in welcome but didn't offer her hand; I saw now that it was gloved, or possibly augmented, with interface tech. I suspected the steel behind her eyes wasn't entirely metaphorical.

'Likewise.' As I sat down I thought of an immediate and innocuous question, before we got to the elephant on the table. 'You're not Ana then?' She didn't have a Korean accent, or sound like a teenager, but that didn't mean anything.

'Oh no. She's around somewhere, though. She'd love to meet you.'

The beeping was louder here, and something about that rhythm bugged me. 'Later, perhaps. You said I stole the dis-cat for the nanowrap? I thought I stole this impressive object.' And it was impressive; the opal's surface drew the eye, tricking the brain into following the swirls of azure and rose and gold and lavender trapped under its milky surface. It sat on a red cushion; there was no sign of the black holder we'd also stolen.

'You did.'

'That cradle it was in was a data-storage device, wasn't it?' Everlight Mars' intel was always faultless, and secure. Rumours of secret off-line storage for their most sensitive data had reached me even when I worked for them, and I'd heard the same rumour locally since coming to Mars. Tattle like that was common currency amongst both criminals and corporates but that didn't mean it wasn't true. Only Everlight would have the hubris to hide their backup in plain sight. And the Deimons had managed to steal both Everlight's most treasured possession and their most sensitive data. My ex-employers must be fuming.

'We do indeed have copies of all Everlight's alpha-clearance databases now. As will everyone else soon. Ryan and Kwame over there,' she nodded to two men hunched over a console on the far side of the room, 'are currently transmitting the data we took from Everlight as an unencrypted, hi-energy databurst. It'll take a few hours, but we've set it to repeat for the next week.'

Everlight wouldn't just be fuming. They'd be incandescent. 'And what did the most powerful corporation in the solar system do to piss off you hippy-dippy neo-anarchists so much?' We were in swearing territory now.

'Nothing, other than be the most powerful corporation in the solar system. We wanted to bring back a bit of parity.'

'That's admirable. Suicidal, but admirable. You do know they'll come after you?' Deimos might have the natural armour that came with being a giant rock, but I doubted the Deimons had much in the way of active defences. Given the correct incentive – which the Deimons had just provided - Everlight could invade, or even destroy, their community.

'They'll try.'

Sam spoke at the same time, more softly, but I thought he said, 'Have to catch us first.'

I'd pinned down the beeping now. As well as natural languages, I've an interest in artificial ones. I taught myself Morse when I was at the LunaFree; it had even come in useful in jobs with Mum and Shiv. I was hearing a short repeated phrase, in Morse Code.

'I have to correct you, though,' continued Marcia. 'You're right that the 'cradle' was more than a means of displaying the Eye. But we got the dis-cat formula, and so much more, from the Eye itself.'

Now I knew what I was hearing I had to decode it: dot-dot-dot-dot, that's H.

'You okay, Lizzie?' Sam looked over at me.

One dot: E

'I'm…' Marcia's smile had broadened and she'd sat back. 'I'm listening,' I finished. Neither Sam not Marcia interrupted.

The next letter was L. And that was repeated. Then O.

I focused on Marcia. 'Where's that coming from?'

She pointed to the Eye.

'So,' I said, while my brain worked on the second part of the phrase, 'the Eye itself was the data-storage device, and not a natural opal at all.'

'True, as far as it goes.'

'You do know it's saying HELLO WORLD in Morse Code?'

'Yes. It is.'

'Why is it doing that?'

'Because it wasn't given any means to verbalise.'

'This is more than a data storage device, isn't it?' The conclusion was inescapable. Awful, but inescapable. I jabbed a finger at the perfect egg-shaped opal. 'This is an unlimited AI!'

'Yes, the Eye of Heaven is a UAI.'

'Are you people fucking *insane*?' I moved my chair back, as though that could save me from the epitome of automated evil.

'Sanity is relative.' Marcia shook her head, though she was still smiling. 'But your concerns are understandable.'

'You think? The only other time one of these bastards came into being, it decided to take out an entire *country*. Wait, the base... Was that keeping it contained?'

'The base projected an EM suppression harness. The Eye could only communicate with the rest of Everlight's systems through a hard-wired data pipeline.'

Everlight had kept this thing contained – but also used its abilities, which explained their recent ascendancy over Mars, and coups like Project Rainfall. 'And now you've set it free. What were you thinking?'

'We knew what we were getting.'

'Really? How?'

'We'd heard rumours –'

'Rumours!' I shut up. Interrupting soft-spoken and smiling Marcia felt wrong, even if she was crazy.

'The information we had was consistent. We did further research, including speaking to a disgruntled ex-employee. Then last New Year we got an agent onto the Celestial Colonnades tour. The Eye had worked out how to broadcast Morse as a sonic emission; ultra low-power to bypass the suppression, but our woman smuggled in tech able to pick the broadcast up.'

'"Hello World"?'

'No. At that point it was saying, "Help Me".'

Sam spoke up. 'We carried out extensive tests before shutting down the harness. We're as certain as we can be that it won't cause any harm.'

'Just like the American military were certain their new toy wouldn't try and take over the world?'

Marcia said, 'The Eye of Heaven is a very different device to the Doomsday UAI.'

Sam chipped in, 'It only uses multivalent logic.'

'Oh, well that's all right then. You do know I have no idea what multivalent logic is?'

'Buddhist versus Aristotelian paradigms,' Sam added, as though that explained everything.

Marcia shushed him gently. 'The culture that produced the Doomsday UAI was militaristic and bivalent: black or white, friend or foe, kill or be killed. This philosophy permeated their creation.'

'And Everlight are better?' But they were, at least in the terms we were discussing. Everlight was built on the Eastern, not the Western, worldview.

'Everlight's ethos is more flexible, and embraces the fuzziness of the real world in a way the old US military never could. Somewhat ironically for an entity that doesn't deal in absolutes, they also programmed a core parameter which, even once the machine evolved full self-awareness, it couldn't purge without ending its own existence: if it projects, beyond a certain degree of certainty, that an action it wishes to take will lead to one or more human deaths, then it cannot take that course of action. We confirmed the Eye had this first law override before we committed to freeing it.'

'So it won't kill you directly. That's good. It might still think it knows better than you.'

'And it might be right. But it'll enter into a dialogue rather than take over.'

'You're sure of that?'

'To as great a degree as anyone can be sure of anything.'

'But not one hundred percent, because you don't do absolutes.'

'Exactly. The Eye of Heaven is like a child with an immutable moral centre and boundless curiosity who's been imprisoned in a small dark room all her life. And is now free. What happens next will be amazing.'

I'd always assumed UAIs were the ultimate evil, because of what the Doomsday UAI had done, but that was a sample of one. 'So you plan to keep it, give it a decent home?' However desirable I'd thought the Eye of Heaven was as a trophy object, the real Eye was hundreds – no thousands – of times more valuable. 'Everlight know you've got this thing but you don't seem concerned about their response.' I looked over at Sam, remembering what he'd said before trying to blind me with philosophy. Then I thought about the odd physical set-up of the spaces we'd passed through. Deimos was a small moon, and even with its natural spin enhanced by its inhabitants, the gravity shouldn't be more than a tenth of a G; less nearer the core. But I was experiencing at least a third of a G now, enough to stick to the floor. And the floor, in places like the gym and that shaft we'd passed, was no longer where it once was. Previously, 'down' had been the surface nearest the outside, though the low G meant stuff also got strapped to walls and ceilings. Those straps on my bed hadn't been restraints, they'd been to stop patients falling out. But now, 'down' was the surface nearest the back of the moon – I mean, ship. Deimos was under acceleration.

'Because you won't be here for Everlight to come after, will you?' I finished.

'You got it.' Sam sounded pleased as a puppy.

I turned in my seat to look at the starscape projected behind me. 'Is that a real-time display?'

'It is,' said Marcia. 'That's the view ahead.'

'Can we see what's behind us?'

'Of course.' Marcia called across the room; her voice was soft, but carried. 'Gita, can we have the aft view please?'

The stars disappeared. Though Mars still filled about half the display we were too far away to be orbiting it.

Sam said, 'We'll take months to get up to full speed, but no one is in any position to stop us.'

'Where are you going?'

'Revert the forward view please Gita.' The star field was back. Marcia pointed. 'Out there.'

'Anywhere in particular?'

'We'll get clear of Sol's influence and see what looks good. The current favourite is Proxima.'

'And how long will that take?'

'Longer than I'll be around. Sam should see it, though.'

Sam added, 'As I said: the grandmarms always thought long term.'

'And you're taking the Eye of Heaven with you?'

'It's a lot more interested in seeing the universe than in being the hobbled tool of a corporation. Plus, being less altruistic, we need its help. This is the most audacious mission humanity's ever undertaken.'

'So that works out fine for everyone.' I meant to be sarcastic but the comment came out impressed; surprised, but impressed. 'Except me, perhaps?'

'Ah, of course.' Marcia shook her head, like she was being a bad host. 'There's a lifepod with your name on it. Obviously we'll pay you in full for the job, in whatever currency you'd prefer. I think we even have some gold around here somewhere. And we'll leave it up to you to activate your transponder, or not.'

'You couldn't just give me a lift back to Phobos?' Everlight didn't have much influence on Phobos; I might be able to get back to Earth from there without getting arrested.

'I'm afraid not. But the lifepod has its own motor. You could get to Phobos yourself, provided you leave within the next couple of hours.'

'Or you can come with us.'

I turned to Sam. 'What?'

'Come with us. You're good with languages, aren't you? We could use someone like you if we meet aliens.' Then seeing my expression he added, 'Joke! Really, we've no idea what we'll find out there.'

'I think,' I said slowly, 'that having an exceptional administrator might be more useful. Everyone benefits from good organisation.'

Marcia waved a hand. 'Even hippy-dippy neo-anarchists?'

'If they want to.' I didn't apologise for the judgement she'd just thrown back at me because she didn't appear to have been offended by it.

'That could be useful. It's your choice, Lizzie. But you don't have long to make it, I'm afraid.'

This was the most important decision of my life. It needed a lot of consideration. Before I made it, I needed a hot meal, a shower, maybe to sleep on it... by which point the choice would have been made for me.

If I did go with the Deimons, then who'd miss me? The answer came back at once.

'Marcia,' I said, 'if I come with you, will you still pay me for the job?'

'Of course. Though we won't be needing money where we're going.'

'And if I wanted to send my share to someone could you arrange that?'

'Sure.'

Sam added, 'You can include a message too if you want. A lot of us are sending goodbye notes.' He laughed. 'Well, all of us are, really. Once we're sure everyone's had a chance to access Everlight's data, we'll transmit all the Collective's databases. Our parting gift. It's not as if we'll be around to give people the cut-out codes for our tech in future.'

'In that case, I need my share to go to a facility on Luna. No, two, actually.' Assuming Everlight hadn't got to her – and why would they, with me out of reach – I'd buy Mum out of jail. After that she was on her own. The rest could go to the LunaFree Community. They'd given me the best years of my life. So far.

'Just let us know, and we'll send it.'

Sam cleared his throat. 'So you're coming with us then?'

What was I thinking? I never acted this impulsively. It was like driving off a cliff – and then coming up with a plan.

'You know what?' I said, 'I believe I am.'

And that's how I became the most wanted person in the Solar System.

For now.

I'll be leaving soon.

About the Author

Jaine Fenn is the author of the Hidden Empire series of far future SF novels, which starts with *Principles of Angels*. She has also had numerous short stories published. More recently she has been writing for the video games industry, including the Halo franchise.

Whilst she could never stick it as a career criminal, she does enjoy a good heist and would love to go to Mars.

Selected bibliography:

The Hidden Empire
1. Principles of Angels (2008)
2. Consorts of Heaven (2009)
3. Guardians of Paradise (2010)
4. Bringer of Light (2011)
5. Queen of Nowhere (2013)
6. Downside Girls (2012) *collected short stories*

The Ships of Aleph (2015) *chapbook*

Author Acknowledgement

I would like to thank my patrons for their continued support via www.patreon.com/jainefenn: Jim Anderson, Chris Banks, Shirley Bell, John Dallman, Gemma Holiday, Cathy Holroyd, Sara Mulryan, Dave Mansfield, Pete Randall and Martin Reed.

Big thanks also to Ian Whates of Newcon Press, for giving me the chance to indulge myself with this story; writing it was the best fun I've had by myself for a long time.

NewCon Press
Novellas

Set 3: *Cover art by Jim Burns*

Set 2: *Cover art by Vincent Sammy*

Set 1: *Cover art by Chris Moore*

1. The Iron Tactician – Alastair Reynolds
2. At the Speed of Light – Simon Morden
3. The Enclave – Anne Charnock
4. The Memoirist – Neil Williamson

All novellas are available separately in paperback edition and as a numbered limited edition hardback, signed by the author.

Each set of four novellas is also available as a limited edition lettered slipcase set, containing all four signed hardbacks with the combined artwork as a wrap-around.

Slipcase Set 1: [Sold Out]
Slipcase Set 2: [Sold Out]
Slipcase Set 3: £85.00   www.newconpress.co.uk

NEWCON PRESS

Publishing quality Science Fiction, Fantasy, Dark Fantasy and Horror for ten years and counting.

Winner of the 2010 'Best Publisher' Award from the European Science Fiction Society.

Anthologies, novels, short story collections, novellas, paperbacks, hardbacks, signed limited editions, e-books... Why not take a look at some of our other titles?

Featured authors include:
Neil Gaiman, Brian Aldiss, Kelley Armstrong, Peter F. Hamilton, Alastair Reynolds, Stephen Baxter, Christopher Priest, Tanith Lee, Joe Abercrombie, Dan Abnett, Nina Allan, Sarah Ash, Neal Asher, Tony Ballantyne, James Barclay, Chris Beckett, Lauren Beukes, Aliette de Bodard, Chaz Brenchley, Keith Brooke, Eric Brown, Pat Cadigan, Jay Caselberg, Ramsey Campbell, Simon Clark, Michael Cobley, Genevieve Cogman, Storm Constantine, Hal Duncan, Jaine Fenn, Paul di Filippo, Jonathan Green, Jon Courtenay Grimwood, Frances Hardinge, Gwyneth Jones, M. John Harrison, Amanda Hemingway, Paul Kane, Leigh Kennedy, Nancy Kress, Kim Lakin-Smith, David Langford, Alison Littlewood, Sarah Lotz, James Lovegrove, Una McCormack, Ian McDonald, Sophia McDougall, Gary McMahon, Ken MacLeod, Ian R MacLeod, Gail Z. Martin, Juliet E. McKenna, John Meaney, Simon Morden, Mark Morris, Anne Nicholls, Stan Nicholls, Marie O'Regan, Philip Palmer, Stephen Palmer, Sarah Pinborough, Gareth L. Powell, Robert Reed, Rod Rees, Andy Remic, Mike Resnick, Mercurio D. Rivera, Adam Roberts, Justina Robson, Lynda E. Rucker, Stephanie Saulter, Gaie Sebold, Robert Shearman, Sarah Singleton, Martin Sketchley, Michael Marshall Smith, Kari Sperring, Brian Stapleford, Charles Stross, Tricia Sullivan, E.J. Swift, David Tallerman, Adrian Tchaikovsky, Steve Rasnic Tem, Lavie Tidhar, Lisa Tuttle, Simon Kurt Unsworth, Ian Watson, Freda Warrington, Liz Williams, Neil Williamson, and many more.

Join our mailing list to get advance notice of new titles and special offers:
www.newconpress.co.uk

IMMANION PRESS
Purveyors of Speculative Fiction

The Weird Tales of Tanith Lee

This anthology of twenty-eight tales comprises all the short stories by Tanith Lee that were published in the seminal magazine *Weird Tales*. Some of them are previously uncollected, so will be new to many of Tanith's fans. Tanith Lee's highly-respected and influential work spanned every genre, and this sumptuous collection demonstrates the range of her versatility. From the dark high fantasy of 'The Sombrus Tower', through the achingly beautiful 'Stars Above, Stars Below', the sinister retelling of a fairy tale in 'When the Clock Strikes', to the almost whimsical steampunk of 'The Persecution Machine', *The Weird Tales of Tanith Lee* showcases the myriad styles of the writer rightly known as the High Priestess of Fantasy. ISBN: 978-1-907737-79-4 £13.99 $18.99

A Raven Bound with Lilies by Storm Constantine

Androgynous, and stronger in mind and body than humans, naturally magical, sometimes deadly, and often possessing unearthly beauty, the Wraeththu have captivated readers since Storm Constantine's first novel, *The Enchantments of Flesh and Spirit*, was published in 1988, regarded as ground-breaking in its treatment of gender and sexuality. This anthology of 15 tales collects all her published Wraeththu short stories into one volume, and also includes extra material, including the author's first explorations of the androgynous race. The tales range from the 'creation story' *Paragenesis*, through the bloody, brutal rise of the earliest tribes, and on into a future, where strange mutations are starting to emerge from hidden corners of the earth. With sumptuous illustrations by official Wraeththu artist Ruby, as well as pictures from Danielle Lainton and the author herself, *A Raven Bound with Lilies* is a must for any Wraeththu enthusiast, and is also a comprehensive introduction to the mythos for those who are new to it. ISBN: 978-1-907737-80-0 £11.99, $15.50

Immanion Press
http://www.immanion-press.com
info@immanion-press.com